ALWAYS
jack

Also by Susanne Gervay

Butterflies
I Am Jack
SuperJack
Being Jack

ALWAYS jack

SUSANNE GERVAY

Illustrated by Cathy Wilcox

Kane Miller
A DIVISION OF EDC PUBLISHING

First American Edition 2013
Kane Miller, A Division of EDC Publishing

First published in English in Sydney, Australia by HarperCollins Publishers
Australia Pty Limited in 2010. This North American Edition is published by
arrangement with HarperCollins Publishers Australia Pty Limited.

For information contact:
Kane Miller, A Division of EDC Publishing
P.O. Box 470663
Tulsa, OK 74147-0663
www.kanemiller.com
www.edcpub.com
www.usbornebooksandmore.com

Library of Congress Control Number: 2012953828

Printed and bound in the United States of America
4 5 6 7 8 9 10
ISBN: 978-1-61067-130-9

Two beautiful and loving girls who understand the journey —
Tory Gervay and Nadia Bottari

Chapter 1

Moving: Sunflowers, Thermometers and Underpants

Sunflower. Can you believe that Mum wanted to call our new house *Sunflower*? I like sunflowers. I made a half-edible sunflower once, except it died. My other great scientific experiment didn't die. Jack's *ponto* — a half-potato-onion. I was nearly famous. Mum cooked the ponto and it tasted delicious, except there was one problem. I didn't write down exactly how I did it. So I'm now on a mission to figure it out again. I've just grafted Ponto Number 24. It's looking good. I check it every day. Ponto 24 is in a glass jar on the windowsill next to my bed. It has plenty of sunlight, air and water.

I record Jack's Ponto Number 24 in my scientific record book. *Saturday: One green shoot sprouting. Smells like onion.* I draw a quick sketch.

Back to sunflowers. Calling our house Sunflower could have wrecked my life. For a start, everyone at school would destroy me — "Let's go to Sunflower's place." (I would be *Sunflower.*) "Jack is a stupid sunflower. Oh no, I mean a budding idiot." (Bud — flower — get it?) "What are you doing, Blossom?" (I would be *Blossom.*) See?

My mum, nanna and sister, Samantha, all love flowers, so they thought Sunflower was a "gorgeous" name. That's Mum's dumb word. It's horrible. The more I said Sunflower is a *bad* name, the more Mum and Samantha giggled and danced around the house doing jumping jacks and singing.

"Sunflowers are lovely.
Sunflowers look nice.
Sunflowers will make our house
Like sugar and spice."

Nanna didn't sing because she's half-deaf and thought everyone was having a great time. I *wasn't.* Luckily my stepdad-to-be, Rob, interrupted them. "I'm planting sunflowers in the garden." Mum and Samantha stopped singing. They liked that idea.

"That'll be enough sunflowers around here. What's another name for the house?" Rob winked at me.

Mum thought about it for a while. "Jack, you really don't like the name?"

"*No*, Mum." I shook my head. Mum didn't get it. I'd be the butt of every joke at school. It's not like I mind a joke, but it's not funny.

Mum's blond fuzzy hair frizzed. "Jack, I want you to like our house name." So the house is now called "Sea Breeze." Mum and Samantha painted blue ripples around the name. I painted a dolphin between the ripples. Samantha loves dolphins. It was amazing on our last vacation. These dolphins came out of nowhere and started surfing with me. Samantha was wearing the dolphin necklace Rob gave her. I copied the dolphin onto the wall. Mum and Samantha said that it looked terrific.

You can smell the salt in the air from our house. It's only a ten-minute walk to the beach. We're around the corner from Napolis' Super Delicioso Fruitologist Market as well. Mr. and Mrs. Napoli and Anna Napoli live at the back of their fruitologist market. Anna is twelve like me and my nearly best friend. She's really my equal best friend. Sometimes she's my best, best friend. I'd never tell her that.

I love our new house. Hector, my white rat, loves it too. It's so much bigger than the place we used to live in. Hector has heaps of room and lives on his own shelf. Sea Breeze has a backyard and a garage with a workshop. Rob and I set up our workbenches and I nailed a board to the wall to hang my hammers, chisels, pliers and screwdrivers.

Rob made a special workbench for Leo, his other son. Rob spent ages putting it together. It's even got a vise to hold wood when you need to cut a piece. I haven't got a vise on my workbench. Rob said I can use Leo's. But this is my house, not Leo's. Leo doesn't even like working in the shed. I can't say anything to Rob. Rob and Mum tell me all the time that I'm the same as Leo. But I'm not. Leo is his real son. Rob's my stepdad-to-be. He says he's already my stepdad. I can't remember my real dad. I'm glad Leo lives with his mother up the coast, which is hours away. I stack my drill and parts on Leo's workbench.

Anyway, I don't care about Leo and he can't fix anything. I screwed three dream catchers into the ceiling for Mum in the big front room. That's Rob and Mum's bedroom. The crystals catch the light through the window and make rainbows across the walls. When the feathers flutter Mum says they are catching hopes and dreams. Rob nudges me and we both try not to smile. Poor Mum is so emotional.

My bedroom is at the back, so I can get to the workshop quickly. It's got an extra bed that I can pull out when a friend sleeps over. It's really good. Samantha has the smallest room, but she doesn't mind. She knows I need space for my experiments and I'm not that neat. Samantha is neat. Floppy, her stuffed flat dog, sits neatly on her neat bed. I stick my head into her room. It's dog-mania in there: puppy posters, Floppy, the A-plus dog project, her dog-eared (joke — ha-ha) *Talking Dog* books stacked in her bookshelf. Puss is curled on her bed. I tease her. "If we get a dog, Puss will love it. A dog will love Puss even more. As dog food."

"Jack, you're mean. I want Mum and Rob to get me a puppy."

I pretend to eat Puss's tail. Samantha chases me out of her room. "You're not funny, Jack."

If Mum and Rob don't get Samantha a puppy, I think she'll need serious medical help. Puss will just have to get used to the competition.

"Nanna," I call out. She lives with us since her bad fall last vacation. She has to get a bone-density scan to make sure her bones don't break so easily. Nanna says I can go with her when she gets her bone scan. Her room is the old porch that's been glassed in. She loves it because the sun streams through the windows and the warmth helps her arthritis. She can see the garden as well. I stomp into her room. She's asleep in her armchair with her mouth open, flashing her set of teeth. There's a snort and her teeth do a flip-flop in and out of her mouth. I try not to laugh, but dash to my room to grab my camera. *Click* — Nanna's mouth is wide-open. *Click* — Puss has jumped into her lap. *Click* — she's chuckling in her sleep. This is hilarious.

Rob said that I'm the official photographer of the move into Sea Breeze. He bought me an excellent digital camera. I have an old-fashioned camera too, and a darkroom at the back of the workshop. Still, a digital is really easy to use and I've been working on editing photos on the computer. I've taken fantastic photos moving into Sea Breeze.

It was crazy when Nanna unpacked her bargain purple underpants. She got them for 50 percent off the 50 percent half-price sale. Wish she hadn't gotten purple underpants for the rest of us, but Nanna loves her sales. Nanna put the underpants on her head. "Everything is covered now," she chuckled. (I get my excellent joke-making talent from Nanna.) Of course, Mum stuck a pair on her head, then Samantha copied. Mum and Samantha chased Rob around the family room with a *big* pair of purple underpants until they landed on his head too. Poor Rob. *Click, click*. I was laughing so hard that the photographs are double exposed, with underpants everywhere.

Rob hung four thermometers in the house. We like thermometers. A house isn't a home unless you know the temperature in every room, according to Rob. It's true. "The weather is just right," he said after checking. "Not too hot and not too cold." *Click*. Photo. Rob's prickly head is nodding at the thermometer. Samantha made me take five photographs of her stuffed dog — Floppy on her bed, Floppy on her desk, Floppy on her carpet, Floppy and Puss in Nanna's lap. Just Floppy — a portrait photo. Samantha *has* to get a dog soon.

It has been hard work moving into Sea Breeze. I had to fix leaking washers and shaky drawers. Grandad was a plumber. I have a whole bookshelf of plumbing and fix-it books. Rob bought me a wrench set and showed me how to fix our leaking toilet. Mum says I'm her plumber. Rob goes around the house banging pipes with his hammer. He thinks *he* is Mum's plumber. But I am.

Luckily I have Grandad's toolbox. Except for Rob, no one else is allowed to touch it. Every tool is in its right place. Every nut and bolt has a home. I'm checking out my toolbox when I discover something missing. The Phillips screwdriver. I feel my face turning red. I bet it is Samantha. I grit my teeth.

Rob scratches his prickly head. Mum twirls her fuzzy blond hair. Nanna says she'll buy me another screwdriver. But it was Grandad's. He wanted me to have it. I charge into Samantha's room. She's sitting next to Floppy braiding her hair as if nothing has happened. "Where's my screwdriver?" I shout.

No answer, but Samantha looks guilty. I am just about to squash Floppy when Mum does a jumping jack into the room with the screwdriver in her hand. "Sorry, Jack. My fault. I used it for an emergency." Mum squeezes Samantha's arm. I can just hear her whisper, "Our secret." They both stare at the dream catcher screwed on Samantha's bedpost. It's obvious that Samantha took the screwdriver. Mum is covering for her. I flick Samantha's dream catcher as I stomp out. "Next time, ask."

Mum usually works Saturday at the library, but she has today off. Sometimes she gets afternoons off and she picks us up from school. I like that. She's a library assistant as well as studying part time to get a library degree. We're really proud of her. I'm glad she's home today. She knows I'm a great dish-washer, ever since Rob let me join his Batman team. We're the washing-dishes super duo, like Batman and Robin. Fast and fantastic. Rob makes the plates sparkle so much that I need sunglasses. Ha-ha.

My specialty is Saturday morning scrambled eggs. Rob isn't a great cook, although his orange juice is excellent. He squeezes the best oranges. But his eggs are a problem. They are either too sloppy or hard like chicken poop. Mum and Samantha are the best chefs, but not for breakfast. I hand Mum a plate with fluffy yellow scrambled eggs, two crispy bacon rashers, sliced tomato on the side and buttered whole-wheat toast.

"You're so clever, Jack." Mum smiles. Nanna nods with yellow bits sticking out of her teeth. Rob sneaks me a quick grin.

"This is good, Jack." Samantha gives Puss a bit of her bacon.

"Hi," echoes through the kitchen. It's Anna. She climbs up the back steps carrying a dripping brown bag. "Over-ripe bananas." They're from Napolis' Super Delicioso Fruitologist Market. Anna's chocolate-brown eyes twinkle. My face flushes.

Anna gives Nanna a hug. Nanna loves that. Then she gives Mum the bananas. There's going to be some serious banana-cake baking this morning. Rob's stacked the plates already. Boiling hot water, forks and knives in line, plates piled, ready for the dish-washing operation. Dishes are washed and wiped and stacked and stored. I help him. Rob stands back to check his work. "Good job," he says to himself. Rob is funny.

Rob waves toward the garden: we're planting the sunflowers. "Coming, Jack?"

"In a minute." I need to check out the big banana bake-off first.

"You can go, Jack." Samantha has her head in

the fridge. "This is for the girls." I ignore her. I love banana cake. Nanna sits in her favorite armchair eating a banana. She drips some of the soft yellow bits onto her clean shirt. I can't watch, but Mum wipes it off. Samantha produces the secret ingredient from the fridge. Mango yogurt. I grab a spoon. "Don't eat the yogurt." Samantha shoots me a serious look. I laugh, stick my spoon quickly into the tub and gulp down a big mouthful.

Samantha grabs the tub away from me, then gives me an evil look. A flick of yogurt hurls across from her mixing spoon and hits my hand. Mum doesn't even see it. Nanna's concentrating on her banana. That's it. I pull Samantha's braid. She squeals, "Don't, Jack, don't." Anna shakes her head, making her licorice curls bounce.

Mum sings out, "Go away now, Jack." The girls, including Nanna, put their hands on their hips and stare at me.

It's so unfair, but hey. I don't want to make the banana cake; I want to eat it. I head for the backyard. Rob's in the garden. He leans on his shovel, then rubs his head. "Getting the soil ready. For the sunflowers."

"Good one." I grab the other shovel.

Chapter 2

What Smells?

Rob and I are packing our shovels away in the shed when Anna calls us from the back door. "Banana cake."

I race up the stairs. The smell is delicious. Banana cake feasting starts seriously. Nanna's in heaven with crumbs dotting her chin. I wave a slice at Anna. "Napolis' Super Delicioso Fruitologist Market is the best."

"We're lucky, Anna, that your family are our friends and neighbors." Mum bites into a slice of banana cake. "It's kind that your parents are doing the fruit for the wedding."

Oh no. The wedding. That word. *Wedding.* Danger, danger, danger. Rob and Mum's wedding.

The most boring topic on earth. I start making chomping sounds. "The cake is great." I grab Puss. She squeals. Samantha is talking about what she'll wear in her hair. I tell a Puss joke. "What happened to Puss when she swallowed a ball of wool?" Pause. "She had mittens."

No laughs. It's like I've said nothing. Anna joins in about the hair. "I was thinking of flowers. Maybe small roses." Groan.

Can't stop it. Mum's excited about the wedding cake. "Christopher's parents are baking the wedding cake just the way we want it."

I know, I know. We *all* know. There're three layers and Mum wants to put Rob as a miniature surfer on the top with herself in a hippie caftan dress. It's the dumbest idea ever. Nanna gets tears in her eyes because Grandad won't be at the wedding. (She misses him. I miss him. I love visiting him at the cemetery.) Then Nanna starts choking and her teeth jump out. I shut my eyes. There's banana stuck in them. Nanna's choking stops, but the wedding doesn't.

I'm happy about Rob and Mum getting married, but why does everyone have to talk about it all the time? It'll be in our backyard with a tent and flame lights and sunflowers now. The wedding cake will be great, and we're going to eat it, OK? Anna and

Samantha are the flower girls. I don't care about what flowers are in their hair or the color of their shoes or if their dresses are going to flounce or not.

There's the worst part. Mum's forcing Leo and me to look like penguins in bow ties and suits. That's scary. Leo will be my official stepbrother or steppenguin. Mum says our bow ties will be floral, so we won't be penguins. I don't want to be a penguin. I really don't want to match Leo either.

"We're going shopping tomorrow," Mum announces. "To buy more things we need for our wedding clothes. Anna and Samantha need shoes. And Jack darling, you're coming too."

"Don't call me darling, Mum." I've told Mum a hundred times not to call me darling — especially at school.

"But you are my darling."

"Mum." I'm going to leave home if she says it one more time.

Rob looks at me. "Got to get back to the garden. Sunflowers." He winks again.

I follow Rob out the back door. I'm not going shopping for more boring wedding clothes.

It's late when Samantha and I walk Anna home to Napolis' Super Delicioso Fruitologist Market. "The sunflowers will look lovely in the garden."

Anna's voice tinkles like bells. No one else's does. Samantha is carrying cake Mum wrapped up for Mrs. Napoli. Mr. Napoli is standing outside the Fruitologist Market polishing a green apple. When he sees us, he bursts into song. Humming in tune, Mrs. Napoli waddles outside. Anna's mum loves the banana cake and gives Samantha a gigantic hug. Luckily I escape. Anna's giggling and waving goodbye to us. Her dimples flash and her licorice hair curls into a twirl.

"Anna's beautiful, isn't she, Jack?"

I don't answer Samantha. Anna is beautiful.

Home. I head for my room to check out my rat. He races toward the cage door. "Come on, Hector." I put him on my lap and his white tail lies on my knee like a shoelace. Hector loves his ears scratched, but he loves Nanna's chocolate chip cookies even more. Rats really like chocolate. He eats the chocolate bits from my hand, but he's not allowed to eat too many.

Samantha sticks her nose in my room. "Are you going to clean up your room before Mum comes in? She found three pairs of underpants under your bed last week." Samantha holds her nose, which is annoying.

"It's none of your business, Samantha."

"Mum said that you're growing an underpants

tree under your bed. Your room smells." She points at Hector. Samantha wiggles her nose now.

I sniff Hector. He smells like grapes, but there's a fishy smell somewhere. It's not the rat. It's not my ponto. My ponto is huge and growing. Oh, I spot it. It's my other experiment — the fungus-in-a-jar on the bookcase. It's looking sick. Maybe even dead. I head for the backyard. I'm going to have to bury it.

Morning. Sun blinks into my room. I jump out of bed and push the curtains aside. I've things to do: record my ponto experiment, work on editing my photos, make Hector a wooden rat-house for his chocolate chip cookie store. But breakfast first. Mum's jumping around the kitchen. Rob's squeezing oranges. Puss is in Nanna's lap. Samantha's showing another drawing of a puppy to Nanna and Puss. Breakfast is fast because there's a lot to do today.

Rob's already at the sink with his yellow plastic gloves. I'm stacking dirty dishes on the counter when Anna arrives at the back door. She's wearing her angel T-shirt. Her silver wings sparkle and tingles race down my back. "Keep your eyes on the dishes." Rob jabs me with his elbow. I ignore Rob. He's dumb sometimes.

Anna's arrived for the wedding shopping trip.

Samantha runs up to her. Mum twirls her red hibiscus skirt. She dances to Nanna's room and brings back a cardigan. Mum helps Nanna put the cardigan on because her hands are too sore from arthritis this morning.

Rob whistles. "I'm the luckiest man alive. Three beautiful girls." Then he looks at Nanna. "I mean four."

Nanna's face beams. "The cardigan is very nice."

I give him a scrunchy stare. He nudges me. "Jack and I have a lot to do. So you girls have a great time at the shops."

Mum flattens her hibiscus skirt and her lip quivers. "But you're coming with us." Rob starts to object, but then he looks at Mum. He knows that Mum-look. It's a you're-hurting-me look. Rob's face drops.

"Not so lucky now," I whisper in his ear.

Everyone piles into Rob's nearly new four-wheel drive Land Rover. Fits all of us in. I help Nanna struggle into the front seat. Mum doesn't mind being replaced in the front. It makes it easier for Nanna. Rob drives to the shopping center and parks next to a huge mobile van. Mum reads the sign aloud. "Free Breast Screening."

"Mum, shush. People will hear you."

Mum's embarrassing, but she doesn't care. "My

17

aunt had breast cancer. I must get around to having a checkup."

Luckily Nanna trips over her shoelaces and Mum gets sidetracked. She holds Nanna's arm and we head for her favorite dress shop and the hippie section. The shop assistant is nearly blinded by the hibiscus skirt and daffodil top as Mum dives into the racks, dragging us behind her. "We need something lovely for the girls." Rob's not allowed to see what Mum's going to wear for the wedding. It's going to be a big surprise.

The fashion parade isn't very lovely. Crazy is a better word. Anna doubles over laughing after jumping out of the dressing room wearing a dotty red dress with crinkly swirls everywhere. She looks like she got measles then sat on a tomato. Rob gets Nanna a chair to watch everything from. Then he leans against the wall and I lean next to him.

The girls try on everything from off-the-shoulder lily tops to snapdragon skirts (really vicious looking) to droopy pansy jackets and white-rose tops. Then Anna glides out in this dress. She shines as she parades around the shop. "The peach blossoms are beautiful." Nanna puts her knobbly hands on her heart. The soft peach makes Anna's black curls and dark eyes sparkle. Samantha tries on the same dress and the girls flounce around the shop and Mum says that they're both princesses.

"Hey, what would it take to make princesses perfect?"

I was going to say something smart like "brains," but Anna's hands are on her hips. Everyone is looking at me. Danger. Danger. I flash a grin. "Nothing."

"Oh, isn't that lovely." Nanna smiles. "The girls are really perfect."

Rob winks. "Just got out of that one, Jack."

Nanna needs the bathroom ten times. Anna can't decide what shoes to get. They're thinking of buying see-through scarves. Mum is secretly looking at the ugliest frock in the world for her dress. I can't take it. Mum glances at me. "This is taking a while. We'll look at bow ties next and then maybe it's enough for you boys."

Yes, yes, we'll be out of here … but bow ties? Can't Mum and Rob just elope? But Mum chooses the worst bow ties ever. "They'll match the peach dresses. There are petals on them." I don't care. I don't care. Let's go home. Home. My ponto needs me. Hector needs me.

"Nanna's tired," Mum says. I give Nanna a grateful look. "We should go home now."

Rob and I are so fast, we really are the super duo. Nanna's whizzed into the front seat. Shopping's quickly stacked in the back. The girls belt themselves in and we're zipping out of the parking lot.

Shopping morning over. Mum disappears into her room. She has a library assignment to finish. Then Rob waves us all over. It's a secret mission that Mum doesn't know about. Samantha has been bothering Rob for ages about this. No, it's not a puppy. Poor Samantha is going to have to keep drawing puppies until she's one hundred and one. I think she's growing a waggy tail and pointy ears. Ha-ha.

"What's so funny?"

"Woof." I laugh, then look at Anna. "Nothing. Can't a guy have a private joke?"

We follow Rob down the road, around the corner. "Where are we going?" Samantha pants. Pants. Pants. I stick my tongue out and scratch my ears. No one gets it. Dog — panting. Then Rob suddenly stops. We're looking into the pet store window. There are no puppies, but Samantha squeals. The mouse-house in the window has lots of mice running around. Samantha immediately falls in love with Patch. He's light brown with small pointy ears and a long patchy tail. "Pick which one you want."

My mouse is Spot because he has white spots all over. Anna picks the littlest mouse and calls him

Frank. Samantha of course has Patch. We walk out with Patch, Spot and Frank, plastic bowls for their water, ladders, bells, a running wheel, mouse food. We'll use Hector's old cage.

"I love the mice." Samantha puts her hand in Rob's.

Mum's not going to love them. She's scared of mice, which is really dumb. What can a mouse do to you? Nothing. (Actually Mum doesn't like Hector much either.)

We arrive home and head for the workshop. There are things to do. Rob gets Hector's old cage. I construct the wheel. Anna cleans the cage. Samantha unpacks the bowls and toys. Anna spreads sawdust on the cage floor, then sets up their food, water, toys. The cage is ready. We pick up our mice by their tails and drop them in. Frank and Patch are already chasing each other around the wheel. Spot's ringing the bell. I'm taking photos.

Rob heads out of the workshop. "Got to talk to Mum." Poor Rob.

Chapter 3

Mice R Nice

Mum's mad at Rob, but she never stays mad. The mice are allowed to stay — Mum doesn't believe anyone should be homeless. So they live in the hallway on the hall table now. Nanna loves watching them run around. Puss loves watching them too. (Mainly because she wants to eat them, so we have to be careful to lock the cage door.) Anna's mouse, Frank, lives with Patch and Spot. Mrs. Napoli is scared of mice like Mum. But unlike Mum, no one can make Mrs. Napoli un-scared, not even Rob or Mr. Napoli. It means Frank lives at our place. It means Anna visits even more. Mum says that Anna's part of the family.

Nanna always waits for us when we come home

from school. The problem is her ears. I bang and bang on the front door. Nanna can't hear the knocking of course. The TV is blaring so loudly no one can hear anything. "Stop banging, Jack. You're making my head hurt." I ignore Samantha.

I find the house keys. "Nanna, Nanna," I call out. We throw our bags into the entrance hall. Anna turns off the TV and we look for Nanna. There is no Nanna in the family room. No Nanna in her bedroom, but there is snoring coming from the kitchen. There she is with her mouth open and her hair done — fluffed and hard. Her top and bottom teeth are lying on the table. Her skirt is caught on the arm of her favorite armchair and she is flashing her purple underpants. Anna and Samantha giggle. I grab an apple as the girls tiptoe out. Only an explosion will wake her up, so I stomp after them.

We go to check the mice. Anna squeals when she picks Frank up by his tail and drops him in the palm of her hand. I can't stop laughing when Frank leaves a plop. Mice are poop machines. Anna laughs too. I nudge her.

"Knock, knock."

"Who's there?"

"Frank."

"Frank who?"

"Frankly, not a poop."

Everyone cracks into laughter. Then it's work time. I take out the mice and put them in a cardboard box. Anna and Samantha start to clean the mouse-house. I hang around for a bit, but I have stuff to do. "I've got to check my ponto."

"You *never* clean *anything*, Jack. It's unfair. You have to help clean the mouse-house!" Samantha flips her ponytail at me.

"I've got scientific experiments to record." I shake my head. "Science is important."

Nanna's awake now and wobbling toward us. "Jack is such a clever scientist."

"Jack's clever all right, Nanna. At getting out of work."

I make a face at Samantha, until I see Anna. I look serious. "I've just got a few things to do. I'll be back soon." Anna gets very focused when she's in the middle of a job. She won't notice I've gone.

I check the fridge, squeeze some oranges, have a drink and take some more photos of my ponto. Then I'm back in the hallway carrying the cardboard box with the mice. The mice like the clean mouse-house with new sawdust and little pieces of apple Anna left in their food bowl. Nanna's face shines as she adds a nibble of cheese. I've told Nanna that mice are not allowed to have cheese because it makes them too fat. Nanna's beaming. I guess it's OK as a special treat.

Rob's Land Rover veers into the driveway. We race to the front door. A hand waves from the car window. It's Mum's, then I see Rob's head and laugh. It's more prickly than usual. He's had another one of his special haircuts. I feel my head. Maybe I need one too. As he gets out of the car, Samantha runs to him and tries to scratch his prickles.

"Hey, watch out. You could mess it up." Rob tickles her stomach. Then he winks at Anna.

I bound across the lawn. I've got to tell Rob about how fast my ponto is growing. He didn't believe I could make it again. "Get out of the way, Samantha."

Rob and I grab the groceries from the car. Mum is in the kitchen already. She made pasta on the weekend, so she just has to heat it up for dinner. I'm starving. Plates set, glasses out, salad cut and chopped and overflowing its bowl. Bread and butter. Nanna is waiting in her chair. Anna sits in the guest spot at the table next to me. The smell of melting cheese and tomatoes puffs through the air and I try not to dribble. Mum piles everyone's plates.

I've got a mouthful of pasta when Rob blurts out, "Leo's staying next weekend." Rob glances at me. "We can go surfing. Surf report says there'll be good conditions."

I love surfing. But Leo? My stomach sinks. Leo's everywhere these days. Mum put two photos of him on the fridge door. One in his school uniform and one baby picture, next to baby photos of Samantha and me.

"I always wanted more kids. I love you visiting, Anna. And there's Leo now." Mum looks at the

photo-covered fridge. Her eyes go watery. Oh no, I can feel a sentimental moment coming. I can't take it and try to detour her. "Great salad."

Samantha butts in. "Oh, that's a cute picture of Puss and Nanna. Hey, Mum, look at that photo of you and Jack." Mum's eyes stop on the photo of her holding me after I was born. Her eyes are getting even more watery. Danger, danger. Nanna is concentrating. Is she going to tell that dumb fish story when I swallowed a fish and pooped it out? I was only two. Nanna coughs. No story, it's just a bit of bread caught in her teeth. The bread's out now.

Mum is looking at my baby photo. She puts down her fork. "Did you know that Jack didn't want to be born?"

I groan. "Mum, we've heard this before."

"Anna hasn't." Mum smiles.

"She doesn't want to," I pipe up.

"I do, Jack." Anna's a traitor.

"Me too." Samantha squiggles next to Rob. She loves hearing this dumb story again and again.

That's all the encouragement Mum needs. "Well, Jack was having such a great time in my stomach, he just decided to stay inside getting bigger and bigger. He was setting up a workshop." Everyone laughs. "Jack was hammering shelves inside me. He gave me a horrible stomachache."

Can Mum stop? I yell out a joke. "Doctor, doctor, what can I do? I swallowed a hammer!

"Doctor answers. Use a screwdriver instead."

Mum ignores the joke. "Jack swam around, eating, experimenting. Jack and his hammer had to be dragged out of my stomach. He came out like a banana head." Mum starts laughing.

I can't help laughing too. "Not everyone can look like a banana head."

Rob pokes me. "That's why Jack's bananas." Everyone is moaning when Rob suddenly gets a bright idea. "Do you know what happened when Leo was born?" No one wants to hear about Leo. "He wasn't born with a hammer. He was born with a hose."

"What are you talking about, Rob?" I kick the rug.

"He came out and sprayed the doctor."

"Leo peed on the doctor." Samantha giggles.

That isn't funny and I don't care. Mum hugs Samantha. "You were beautiful when you were born. Even though you had no eyelashes." Samantha was born too early, which is why she didn't have any. I don't want to hear this story again. Mum's gone all soppy. I guess it's better than talking about Leo.

"She has eyelashes now." Anna hugs Samantha too. Oh no. Mum extends her arms to me. I shake my head. I'm not joining in.

"They put Samantha under special lights with a black blindfold over her eyes and fed her through a tube in her nose." More tears dot the corners of Mum's eyes.

I roll my eyes. "Good that everyone was born, Mum." I put my you've-got-to-be-joking tone into it. No reaction. I glance at Anna. Definitely glad Anna was born, but this has to stop. Tactical response. Change the topic. Mice. They love talking about mice. "Hey, everyone. The mice need feeding." I'm right. The mice discussion starts. Samantha likes their games. (My Spot is the best acrobat.) Mum thinks they smell. (They do.) Nanna still wants to give them cheese. Even Rob adds that mice don't eat much. Saved by the mice.

Then Samantha asks the dumbest question. "Do you think the mice should meet Hector?"

"No," I shout at Samantha who knows nothing about survival of the biggest. Hector is a good rat, but he'd kill Patch, Spot and Frank.

Leo's staying this weekend. Mum has ordered me to clean my room. I don't see why I have to. Mum told Samantha that she has to help me. I don't want her to. My head is thumping and she's humming. I grit my teeth. "Stop humming." She doesn't. I ignore her.

There's Wally, the one-eyed stuffed cane toad on the floor. I dust him and stick him at the back of my cupboard. Cane toads have been eating our green frogs and making it hard for our honeybees. I don't like Wally much anymore. I slump onto my bed.

Finally Samantha stops humming. "Are you all right, Jack?"

I don't say anything. She just hangs around like a bad smell. "Go away, Samantha."

She sits on my bed. "Did you hear me? It's Leo, isn't it?"

"It's none of your business. Why don't you go and do your hair?"

"Leo's all right."

Can Samantha be quiet? "It's not like Leo's going to live here. Anyway, Rob is our dad."

My throat is dry. Once I called Rob "Dad," and he made a joke about it. Samantha calls him Dad sometimes and Leo calls him Dad all the time, but not me. I don't care because Rob and I are mates. It's not like I need a father. I don't want a father. My head is throbbing.

Oh no, Nanna is shuffling along the hallway toward my room. I don't want Nanna to be here now. Go away, Nanna. I stare at Nanna trying to make her leave. But she just keeps shuffling in and when she says hello, I see that she has left her bottom teeth somewhere again. Nanna plunks herself onto my chair. "Nanna, I've got to clean up my room." I jump off my bed and grab my waste-paper basket. Samantha picks up the overflowing one and we head for the outside garbage can. When we come back Nanna is still sitting there. *Go away*, I want to shout at her.

Nanna smiles. "You are such a wonderful boy, Jack." She looks at Samantha. "And you are a wonderful girl. I am so lucky to have you both." Her green eyes sparkle and I feel like a rotten person and Leo is coming.

Chapter 4

Surf's Up

Another Saturday morning. A car pulls up and I race to the family room window. Samantha squashes next to me and Mum presses behind us. Spy force, that's us. Just need binoculars to check out what's happening. Rob's gone outside. Leo's standing next to him, carrying his computer games. Leo's mum gets out of the car. She's thin with black hair like Leo. She and Rob are talking and Rob isn't smiling. Leo is staring at his shoes and he's not smiling either. Rob's hand is on Leo's shoulder.

"Can you hear them?" Samantha asks me.

I head to the open front door with Mum and Samantha tagging behind. Nanna can't hear anything, so she stays in her chair patting Puss.

"If you were any type of a father, you'd drive up and see Leo every week," Leo's mother shouts. I can't hear what Rob answers. "Isn't he important to you?"

That's so unfair. She doesn't know anything. Leo *is* important to Rob. I watch Leo standing there looking at his shoes. His face is white. I get this bad feeling in my head. How can Rob drive up to see Leo at Port more than he does now? It's five hours away and Rob works and has us. Anyway, she was the one who took Leo to live up there.

"It's all right for you moving into a new house with a big yard. What about Leo? We live in a tiny apartment."

Rob speaks clearly and loudly, not like Rob at all. "Leo, say goodbye to your mother." He nods at her. "So you'll pick him up tomorrow afternoon." Rob grabs Leo's arm and they walk toward our open door. She slams the car door shut and a man, I guess it's Leo's stepdad, speeds away.

Leo just stands in the family room holding his computer games. We all say "hi" to him. He says "hi" under his breath.

Nanna's green eyes twinkle. "You've grown taller, Leo."

We're all standing around like stuffed tomatoes. I have to do something. "Rob's moved a table into my room for your games, Leo. Do you want to look?" I'd been really angry about the table. I feel like a rat now. That gives me an idea. "Do you want to see Hector?" Leo shuffles after me.

We check out Hector, then my ponto. Leo looks interested before he sets up his computer games. I notice a photo of Leo and his mum on his screen. Guess he loves his mum. I end up working on my new fungus experiment. Leo doesn't talk, but we both look up when Samantha and Nanna arrive with chocolate chip cookies for Hector. "Hector's not allowed so many cookies, Nanna."

She giggles. "Just a little treat." Nanna sprinkles a few broken-up ones in Hector's bowl. Hector loves Nanna. Then she and Samantha head off to give some chocolate chip crumbs to the mice. I give up.

Suddenly Rob's head appears in the doorway. "Are you boys OK?" Leo keeps playing his games. The car scene this morning flashes into my mind. Why is Leo's mum so angry? It's not Rob's fault. It's not Leo's fault either. I feel bad. I'm going to force myself to be Leo's friend, whether Leo likes it or not.

"Pack your things away. We've got work to do. A barbecue."

I like barbecues. Last week, Rob and I set up the barbecue area next to the sunflower patch. It's so good having our own backyard. I give Leo a tour of the shed and show him his workbench and the metal locker. Rob's put Leo's surfing gear there. Leo's looking a bit happier. "No one will touch your stuff here. It's your space." Then I remember Samantha. She could "borrow" something. No, I won't say anything to Leo. He's got enough problems.

It's teamwork. Everyone pitches in bringing out the blue-checked tablecloth, plates and knives, glasses, sausages and steaks, salads, salt and pepper, ketchup. Christopher will be over soon with rolls. His mother is coming which is really rare. His parents hardly ever leave their bakery. Christopher works there most afternoons as well.

Leo's helping Rob get the barbecue going. It's sizzling when Rob throws sausages onto the grill. I yell out, "Hey, Rob, how do you know sausages don't like being fried?" Ha-ha. Rob doesn't know. "Because they spit."

"That's smart, Jack." Rob grins.

"Yep, that's me. Smart."

I grab my camera and click Mum rocking around, Nanna eating cookies, Leo flipping sausages. The Napolis arrive and I click some shots of Mrs. Napoli waving her arms in the air. "The banana cake you sent us was very beautiful." She hugs Mum, who loves compliments. I click so many photos of Anna that she starts laughing, so I take some more.

Christopher and his mum arrive. He's holding up

a ball. We'll play handball this afternoon. Anna quickly says hello, before she and Samantha check out the mice. Someone needs to clean their cage soon. They always smell.

"Come and get it," Rob calls out. Leo's sticking pretty close to him, and I want to hang out with Christopher for now. Mum makes sure everyone has plates, ready for the feast.

I squirt ketchup over the sausages and take some rolls, then Christopher and I head toward the back porch where Nanna is sitting. "Here's a sausage, Nanna." She loves sausages. She doesn't like steak because it's too hard to eat and her teeth slip out. Right away a big blob of ketchup plops onto her blouse. That's Nanna. Her wrinkles crease into a smile. "Your grandad would have loved this." I wish Grandad was here. When we visit him next time in the cemetery, I'll take my ponto and show him. "Where are your grandparents?" Nanna asks Christopher.

I've never thought about Christopher having grandparents. He just goes to school with me, and there's his mum and dad, and he's my mate. (I know Anna has grandparents who live in Italy. The Napolis are planning to visit them next year.)

Christopher takes his handball out of his pocket and squeezes it. I don't think he's going to answer.

"I remember my grandmother. My dad's mother. She lived with us, but died when I was little."

"I'm so sorry, Christopher." Nanna gives a toothy sigh. "And what about your other grandparents?"

"They never got out of Vietnam. Soldiers from the north took them away. No one knows what happened to them."

Nanna reaches out her knobbly hand to Christopher. "Jack's grandfather fought in Vietnam." I've seen Grandad's medals, but I don't really know what happened. "What's your Vietnamese first name, Christopher?"

What first name? Christopher is one of my best friends — I know his name.

"An." Christopher looks really uncomfortable. "It means peace."

How did Nanna know? How come Christopher never told me? He speaks Vietnamese, but never talks about Vietnam. I know he's clever at school and wants to be an engineer and he plays great handball. I didn't know he had another name called Peace.

Samantha and Anna run over with more sausages and rolls. Everyone is too full: even I can't eat another sausage. Mrs. Napoli pours her homemade grape juice into cups and then she says the boring, annoying, dumb word. "*Wedding*." Mum's face lights up and there's a girl huddle with Mrs. Napoli,

Nanna, Samantha, Anna and Mum and they start. "What about the dresses for the wedding?"

Christopher and I give each other the look. We're going to play handball.

I turn around and see Leo. "Do you want to play, Leo?" He looks at Rob and then they both walk over. The side wall of the garage is just right for handball.

Christopher wins two sets and I win two sets. Leo wins one set. "We're pretty good." I pummel Christopher's back. I'm chasing him when his mother calls out that they're going back to the bakery. When we stop, I whisper in his ear. "Are you going to tell me? We're mates, aren't we?" Christopher shrugs, but he knows I'm talking about Vietnam and his name.

"Later." He races toward his mother.

I'm going to ask Nanna about Grandad and Vietnam later too. The Napolis are leaving as well. Mum packs leftover salads and cake for them. Anna waves, but we'll see her tomorrow because she's coming to the beach with us. Rob calls out that he and Leo are walking to the store to buy milk. "We're short of milk," Rob says, but it's a lie. We've got enough milk. I get a shooting pain in my head. Then I look at Mum and Samantha and Nanna. I'm all right.

Sunday morning. Rob walks in with a determined look. He checks the thermometer. "Perfect weather, not too cool and not too hot." He takes out the juicer squisher and six oranges. Glasses are lined up on the kitchen counter. Breakfast is quick with cereal, toast and orange juice. Surf's up and we don't want to waste time.

Leo's ready with his board. I've got mine. Samantha has hers. Nanna stands there in her faded yellow beach dress with her yellow sun hat. "Your grandad loved this dress." She brushes out the creases. Nanna talks a lot about Grandad. We're visiting Grandad at his grave soon.

Mum whirls into the room with *her* yellow sun hat, holding one for Samantha. Nanna loves the sun hats especially since she bought them at Susie's Super Discount Store. Nanna always says she's so clever to have found them. "The best bargain in the shop." Photo opportunity. I snap hats and girls. It's going to be a great shot. We could walk to the beach, but Nanna can't make it that far, so we pile into Rob's car. Anna's waiting in front of Napolis' Super Delicioso Fruitologist Market with Mr. Napoli. Leo and I start laughing. Guess what? She's wearing her yellow sun hat, bought by Nanna.

Everyone's laughing. Nanna knows she's the star and gives a huge toothy grin.

The waves are rolling in. I'm dying to get into the surf, but I have to help Mum move Nanna out of the car. Hurry up, Nanna. Hurry up. We organize a folding chair for her, and the sun umbrella. It takes forever. At last Nanna saves me. "Go have a swim. Stop fussing." I love Nanna. "I'll enjoy the beach and watching you."

Great, we're off. The water is just right. Leo and I head for the waves. Rob follows with Samantha and Anna. Mum stays with Nanna. We wait for a set of waves, then paddle like mad. I get a big one. Leo catches the next wave. It's only a boogie board, but Leo's good. Suddenly he's half-kneeling on his board. Half-drop. I've been trying to do that move for ages. Leo spins the board before riding a small shore-break tube. The waves crash over him as he does a turn. Anna calls out, "Leo, you're terrific."

"Terrific?" I stand on my hands in the surf with my legs in the air. Anna splashes away from Leo to me. Samantha splashes behind her. As I stand up, Anna laughs and her eyes sparkle. Her wet black curls dangle over her ears and my face feels hot. "Hey, what kind of hair do oceans have?" Anna shakes her head. "Wavy. Ha-ha." I'm a funny guy.

"*Not* funny," Samantha squeaks.

"What's small, wet and noisy?" I grab Samantha's toe. "Samantha." The waves roll in and we're off before Samantha can stick her tongue out.

I can't believe that it's already time to leave. We have to be home in time for Leo's mother to pick him up. As we drive home, Leo is quiet. Rob says, "You can stay whenever you want, Leo." That's not really true. Rob knows it's not true. There's school and arguments between Rob and Leo's mother and Leo lives too far away. "I'll come up when I can." Rob knows he can't get away that much. "You'll be here for the wedding. It's soon." That's true.

We drop off Anna. Home, unpacking, showers, Leo's ready just in time. There's a loud car horn beeping. It's his mother. I'm standing with everyone on the front porch. We watch Rob and Leo walk toward the car. Leo's holding his computer games. We wave at him. He quickly opens the back door. He doesn't even give a short wave. Leo looks at Rob through the open car window. I can just hear him say, "Bye, Dad."

Chapter 5

Leftover Sausages

Dinner is leftover sausages and salad. Rob's not speaking and Mum's not bouncing around. Puss is in Nanna's lap and Samantha is patting her.

Leo looked really miserable in the back seat of the car. He's probably halfway to Port by now. Suddenly I feel rotten. I'm going to take my tools off Leo's workbench in the workshop. Then I get an idea. "Rob, in the next school vacation can we go on a surfing trip up north? We can get Leo and camp in the National Park." I glance at Mum. "After the wedding."

"After the wedding," she brushes Rob's hand, "we'll make time for Leo."

Rob leaves the clean dishes to dry, and nudges

me. "Coming, Jack? Got to put away the rest of the barbecue things and all that." We head off to the workshop.

I shove the gas cylinder under the workbench. Rob puts Leo's boogie board in his locker. He's just standing there looking nowhere. "You're a good kid, Jack." Rob never says things like that. He stays frozen for ages. "Leo's a good kid."

I get this pang in my head. I'm not a good kid. Leo isn't a good kid. I'm an all-right kid. Leo's an all-right kid. He's not my best friend, like Christopher. I watch Rob wipe down the workbench. I like Rob here. I like Mum and Rob at home. Leo's mother jumps into my thoughts. She was so angry and Leo's stepfather drives like a maniac and shouts. I don't like it when Mum and Rob go out at night. When Rob comes home late. What if there's an accident? What if they're killed in a car crash? I'd have to take care of Nanna and Samantha and I've got no dad. I shake my head. This is dumb. Nothing will happen to Rob or Mum, but if it did … Nothing will happen.

"I need to see more of Leo." Rob checks the thermometer in the workshop. "Parents can make a mess for you kids." He flicks my head. "We have to get haircuts before the wedding."

*　　*　　*

Monday morning Rob goes early to work as usual. Mum's in the kitchen making school lunches before she leaves for the library. I give Hector a pat, pack my bag, check out my ponto. It's got another green shoot. I quickly write that down in my scientific notebook and take a photo. Need the bathroom. "Samantha, get out of there." I bang on the door. I can hear the hair dryer. She's doing her hair. She's always doing her hair. I bang on the door.

Mum calls out, "Stop that, Jack."

"Samantha is so slow," I shout back.

Mum doesn't answer, but Nanna is shuffling along the hallway. Oh no, I've got to get into the bathroom before Nanna. She takes forever.

Samantha comes out just in time, with her ponytail bobbing. "Hey, Samantha. What did the pony say when Jack grabbed her tail?"

Samantha scrunches up her nose. "What, Jack?"

"That's the end of you." I look at her. "You get it? The end, the tail." She giggles. I quickly pull her ponytail and race into the bathroom. I am so funny.

Today Nanna is walking with us to the school bus stop. She's on an assignment. Christopher's parents' bakery is right next to the bus stop and she needs to buy some cream buns for our after-school "treat." That's what she always calls our buns. She's buying some hot doughnuts for her morning tea "treat" too. She's dropping into Napolis' Super Delicioso Fruitologist Market as well, to get some bananas. Nanna has finally accepted that she's wobbly. She knows that she has to use her walking stick when she goes outside though she still sneaks out without it when no one's looking. She doesn't catch the bus

anymore. It's too dangerous because she can fall. The good part of this is that Nanna can't get to Susie's Super Discount Store in the shopping center — she only shops down the road these days. So she can't buy any more fluorescent-purple underpants. Nanna's bargains are good and bad. I love her buying cream buns, but I don't love her buying purple underpants even if they *are* cheap and amazing.

Christopher and Anna are waiting for us at the bus stop. I take a ball out of my pocket and wave it at them. We're playing at lunchtime. Christopher and our mate Paul have been practicing, but Anna's sometimes better than they are. I'd never tell them. Nanna waits for us to get on the bus, then leans on her walking stick and trundles toward the bakery.

On the bus Samantha and Anna sit in the girl group. George Hamel and his mates are hanging out at the back of the bus. It seems ages ago when he used to bully me. He doesn't anymore. If I see a kid being bullied on the bus, my friends and I hang around the kid. Bullies always pick on kids when they're alone or can't defend themselves. I've been there and it wrecks your life. I'm not scared of George Hamel anymore.

The bus driver screams when he sees an apple core whiz down the aisle. "Who did that?" He's looking around as we clamber off the bus. He grabs a kid by the collar and grumbles that he's going to report him to the principal.

Christopher and I are laughing when we get into our classroom. Mr. Angelou gives us a sit-down-and-keep-quiet stare. Anna passes a note across the aisle. I just see it before Mr. Angelou grabs the paper, looks at it, then throws it in the trash. Anna has sketched her flower-girl dress for the wedding. She's turned red. "Sorry, Mr. Angelou."

The wedding's a month away. Wish it was over and done with already. Rob and I aren't allowed to see Mum's wedding dress, although Samantha, Anna and Nanna have. At least I didn't have to go shopping for it. I couldn't stand another day hanging around dress shops. It's so boring. Anna's coming over this afternoon to discuss more stuff about the wedding with Samantha. What else can they discuss? Anna also wants to visit Frank.

Mr. Angelou writes on the board. "Immigration." It's our topic area for the term, and he's describing our major project today. "I want you to select places that matter to you. Maybe where your family came from, or your ancestors. Or the focus could be on Australia and the first European settlers or New Zealand's Maoris or the Sioux Native Americans — or people from any part of the world. The project will involve research, history, interviews. You can include photos and posters." Mr. Angelou's bald head shines except for the tufts of hair out the sides. "You'll work by yourselves or in pairs."

Anna's chocolate-drop eyes sparkle as she puts her hand up to say she'd like to do Italy. Wish I had my camera. "We'll do Vietnam," I call out, elbowing Christopher.

Mr. Angelou's head shines. "That's a great choice, Anna. You too, Jack and Christopher." Other kids choose Ireland, Greece, Afghanistan, Thailand, Lebanon, Hungary, England, China, Sudan, Israel, the Outback. I didn't know kids from my class came from so many places.

"We're beginning the project today. I've organized books in the library, computers and information to help you get started. You'll work on it at home as well as in class sessions." Mr. Angelou hands out worksheets with all the activities, then helps a few kids who can't decide what they want to do. Christopher and I scramble up the stairs to the library. I'm panting as we race each other to the desk by the window. We leave our stuff there and go to the shelves. We find a great book, *The History of the Vietnam War*. I open up at the first page: it's a map of Vietnam, divided into North and South. "Where's your family come from, Christopher?"

"The South. A village near Saigon."

I flip to a chapter on Saigon: photos with thousands of bicycles and motorbikes and people in long-sleeved tops and flapping trousers, wearing pointed bamboo hats. The description says that the buildings are French with arches and stonework. There are bamboo shutters and laundry hanging out over the old stone balconies. A crinkled man with eyes like Christopher's is bending forward with his hands pressed together. A soldier is bowing with his hands pressed together too. It feels sad. Christopher doesn't say a word.

I flip to pages about the countryside. There are photos of mountains, jungle, rivers, villagers in huts, soldiers in uniforms with machine guns, burned-out trees and planes in the skies. Then I turn the page and there is a photo of a girl. She's running down a dirt road with soldiers behind her and kids in front, screaming with their mouths wide open. *Pulitzer Prize photograph by Nick Ut of nine-year-old girl Phan Thi Kim Phuc fleeing from her village of Trang Bang, June 8, 1972.* She's naked and burning. It's hard to look at the photo. I read the word *napalm*.

Mr. Angelou is leaning over our shoulders. Christopher is leaning over his hands. Mr. Angelou speaks quietly. "Write what you need to, Christopher. And Jack, this is why it's an important thing to be a photographer."

I copy from the book: *The Vietnam War lasted from 1959 to 30 April 1975 when the democratic South Vietnam, supported by the United States, Australia and New Zealand, was defeated by the communist North Vietnam.*

The lunchtime handball game is fast and Christopher thrashes me. That's OK. The photo of the girl keeps flashing into my mind. His family must have been through a lot. We're doing math this afternoon. Mr. Angelou gives us heaps of math homework. I'm fast at math, but Anna isn't. I'll help her this afternoon when she comes over.

"Nanna, we're home." I open the front door. Nanna's waiting for us with cookies and apple juice. Mum's home early today too. I drop my bag and head for the kitchen. Everything's looking good — food set out, bananas cut up from Napolis' Super Delicioso Fruitologist Market *and* cookies. Anna and Samantha go off to check the mice, but I'm starving. My mouth is stuffed when I nearly choke because of the great scream. I'm spluttering out banana and cookie bits when Samantha runs into the kitchen crying. She's pointing to the hallway. "It's in there. In there." She's sobbing. "Patch."

I lead the charge into the hallway. The mouse-house looks all right. Anna's mouse Frank is running around the wheel like an athlete. Spot is crouching in a corner, but when I open the cage he slides into my hand. Then I see Patch. He isn't moving. His small paws are not moving.

Anna and Samantha are holding on to each other. Mum's patting down her hair nervously. It's awful, but I decide to take charge. Everyone is quiet as I carry the mouse-house into the garden. Anna lays Patch in a small box that she has lined with tissue paper. Nanna watches us from the back porch with Puss. I get my spade and dig near the sunflowers. I don't feel like joking. Anna gently puts Patch in the hole and says a few words over his grave. Samantha snuggles in Mum's arms. She hides her face in Mum's shoulder as I bury Patch.

Afterward, we sit on the back porch looking over the garden. Samantha whispers, "Mum, why did Patch die?"

Mum takes a while to answer. "Maybe Patch was sick. Maybe he was already old. Maybe it was just his time."

Suddenly my head hurts. Nanna is sick and old.

"I want Patch here."

"He is here, Samantha." Mum puts her hands across her chest. Samantha lies against her.

"It's not fair. Why do things die?"

Mum strokes Samantha's cheek. "We're born, grow up, are part of the world. It's a gift to be here." Mum's eyes are teary.

"I don't want Patch or anyone to die, Mum."

"Patch has the snug warm earth around him and we love him. And where he's gone is a safe place."

I sit next to Nanna and hold her hand. It's soft and wrinkly and warm. I couldn't stand anything happening to Nanna. "Can we visit Grandad soon?"

Mum nods. Nanna smiles. "I'd like that, Jack."

Chapter 6

Grandad Is a Hero

Samantha puts flowers on Patch's grave and he becomes part of our sunflower garden. "Patch would like that." She sniffs back a sob.

There are heaps of phone calls from Leo. He doesn't want to know about Patch, even though Samantha is really sad. All he wants to talk about is Rob going north, even though the wedding is soon and Rob doesn't have any time. So what's Rob doing? He's taking a day off work on Friday and will be away all weekend. To make up for Friday, Rob has to work overtime. So he'll miss dinner with us and be home late every night. Rob can't work with me on the portable mouse-house for Samantha's school show-and-tell. He promised he would.

"I need some time with Leo," Rob says. "You understand, Jack and Samantha."

Understand? Rob wouldn't take a day off work for me. He just wouldn't. I'm not his real son, so it doesn't matter. But I'm just saying what's happening. Rob made Leo a special workbench, and now he's driving north for the weekend to be with him. I don't care. I don't need his help making the portable mouse-house. The only thing Rob did was give me two heavy-duty cardboard boxes from work.

Every night I've been working on the mouse-house with Samantha as my assistant. Samantha needs to take Spot and Frank to school for her class project on pets. Other kids have brought in lizards, a rabbit, two guinea pigs, frogs and goldfish. Samantha has made a poster of Patch to stick on the side of the mouse-house. "Just because someone dies, doesn't mean they're not here," Mum says and it's true.

Samantha brings me a roll of toilet paper. I unwind it to get the cardboard tube in the middle. (Mum wasn't happy about this.) Then I cut a hole in the small box and slide the toilet paper roll in as a passageway before putting the other end in the side of the big box. Spot and Frank can run from the small box to the big one. It's really comfortable. I glue Samantha's poster onto one side of the mouse-house. It folds in half. You just flick it open to see Patch. On the other side of the box, I've stuck a sign. It's looking good. I carry it into the family room to show everyone.

Nanna puffs up like Wally, my stuffed cane toad. "You're just like your grandad. He could make anything."

"You're the best brother, Jack." Mum puts her arm around Samantha.

"Not bad." Rob checks out how I put it together. "You built it better than I could." He reads my sign aloud.

"DON'T TOUCH.

(WELL, HOLD AT YOUR OWN RISK.

YOU'LL FIND OUT WHAT HAPPENS.)"

Samantha picks up Spot by the tail and then it happens. POOP. POOP. POOP. She giggles.

Mum grins at me and says, "Mice really are POOP machines." Everyone laughs because we all know what happens now. POOP.

It's Friday morning and we wave Rob goodbye. He beeps the horn, sticks his head out of the window and yells, "Be back soon."

Mum reads my mind. "Leo needs to see his dad." I say nothing.

After Rob disappears, Mum talks to us about her plans for today and the weekend. There are so many: organizing Nanna's doctor's appointment in the hospital (scientific); visiting Grandad (I'll show him my ponto); another fitting in my penguin wedding suit (bad, but at least Leo won't be there); and gardening to get the backyard ready for the *huge* wedding (luckily I've got homework). Christopher and I are working on the Vietnam project this weekend. Mum says schoolwork comes first. School. Have to rush. "Come on, Samantha."

"I want to carry the mice by myself." Samantha struggles down the stairs. I take her backpack.

"Let's go!" Anna and Christopher'll be waiting for us at the bus stop. "Come on. No, you can't show Nanna. No time." I look at my watch. Got to move. We're puffing as we round the corner. I call out. Anna and Christopher turn around and wave to us. Luckily, the bus hasn't come yet. They're impressed with the mouse-house. Anna gives Frank a special pat.

She smiles and I catch a flash of her dimples. "Jack, that was really nice of you to make the mouse-house for Samantha."

"It was nothing." But I point out the special designs in the mouse-house. As Anna boards the bus and heads down the aisle, she says, "You're smart as well as nice."

"You're so *smaaart* and *niiice,* Jack." Samantha wrinkles her nose. I grab her arm and squeeze hard. "Ouch, that hurts! Stop it, Jack. You nearly made me drop the mouse-house."

"Next time I won't make you anything."

"Well, don't. We made it together," Samantha huffs as she follows Anna, then plonks herself next to her on the bus. She's so irritating.

Christopher sits next to me behind the girls. Kids are leaning over the bus seats to look at the mice. Frank is the speediest mouse in the house. He makes the wheels turn. Spot's eating, pooping, gnawing on a piece of hanging string. Samantha's drawing of Patch is a hit. Samantha's sign under Patch reads, THREE AMIGOS — FRIENDS ALWAYS. As long as we remember, Patch's still here.

Samantha and the mice have a great day. When the last school bell rings, I wave goodbye to Anna. Mum's outside tooting the car horn. Samantha puts the mice on the back seat next to Nanna. She's in the car ready to go to the hospital for her doctor's appointment. She chuckles. "Guess what I'm wearing?" I don't ask, but I can take a guess. I think they're purple.

Nanna's brought her cards to play UNO. "Sometimes you have to wait a long time in the waiting room." She pauses for effect. "That's why it's called a waiting room."

Jack joke coming. Joke coming. "Doctor, doctor, I feel like a pack of cards." Pause. "Sit down, Nanna, and I'll deal with you later."

Nanna laughs so much her teeth pop out, but she sucks in her breath and they slip straight back in. We play four games of UNO waiting in the hospital. Nanna's name is called at last. Mum goes in with her and as Nanna turns to give us a little wave she flips her skirt and guess what? A flash of fluorescent-purple hits us as she waddles inside. Samantha giggles. I guessed right.

While Mum and Nanna are inside and we're outside, we play another game of UNO and Samantha wins, but I don't mind. We have to bring Nanna back next week for blood test results. Mum's coming in too, to the hospital breast cancer screening clinic for her mammogram checkup. She booked it after she saw the van at the shopping center and because she has to bring back Nanna anyway.

Saturday, first stop, Grandad. Nanna's brought a dish towel to dust Grandad's headstone. Samantha arranges the bright-yellow sunflowers in a jar. Mum brings out the blue-checked tablecloth and lays out rolls and lemonade. I set up the folding chair for

Nanna. It's a bit windy, so I race to the car to get her favorite bargain cardigan.

When we're all comfortable and organized, we tell Grandad about Nanna's bone-density scan, the mouse-house and Patch, Rob going north, the wedding. When I bring out my ponto, Mum gasps because it's huge now. She hasn't seen it for a while. The morning is warm in the sun with gold blinking from the sun hats. Grandad's grave looks out over the blue sea with boats bobbing up and down. I snap photos of yellow and blue and sun hats and Nanna's knobbly hands resting on Grandad's grave. She whispers to him, "We'll be together again one day." Then Nanna strokes the headstone as if he was here. I know she wants to see him, but I don't want Nanna to leave me.

Going home I sit in the back seat holding my ponto. Mum's fuzzy blond hair and Nanna's hard head bob in front of me. They're talking and laughing, but I just feel sad.

Vietnam project. I've set up Rob's video camera; he said I could use it because he trusts me. I have interview questions written down, the computer screen ready for Nanna to see photos, the books on the Vietnam War opened at special pages. Nanna's brought out her photo album and Grandad's special box to help give the answers.

There's a glass of water on the side table in case Nanna gets thirsty. Christopher arrives with three doughnuts and four chocolate chip cookies for the interview. There's one for each of us and an extra cookie for Nanna in case she gets hungry or needs an urgent Nanna "treat." The main thing is that Nanna doesn't fall asleep. Christopher brought a bag of goodies for Mum and Samantha from his parents too.

Nanna's room is set up with her armchair facing the camera. We've pulled down the blinds. "Ready, Nanna?"

"Ready, Jack."

Christopher videos me opening the books and showing photos. It's the introduction. Then he pans to my face. I explain that Grandad fought in Vietnam and that I am interviewing Nanna about what she remembers. "Here's Nanna." She gives a toothy grin and waves to the camera.

I ask the prepared questions. "What was the Vietnam War about?"

"The Vietnam War," Nanna repeats. "Well, Jack, it was like yesterday." Nanna remembers the past better than today. "Well, Jack, everyone was scared of communism."

"What's communism, Nanna?"

"Communism is supposed to be where everyone is equal and the government looks after everyone equally. So there's no need to vote for a new government." Nanna sips some water. "That sounds good, doesn't it, Jack?"

I guess it does.

"But it doesn't work. People are individual and communism tries to make everyone think the same way. People were put in prison, tortured, even killed if they didn't support the government.

"Vietnam was a long and terrible war, Jack. A lot of soldiers died and a lot of Vietnamese people died too. The countryside and villages were bombed and destroyed." Nanna takes another sip of water. Christopher keeps filming. "America and Australia and some other countries went in to fight against North Vietnam. Lots of people didn't want our soldiers there because there were too many people killed. Because it was not in our country. It was hard on our soldiers. The North communists won in the end."

My head pounds. I knew that North Vietnam won. Christopher's family escaped here to get away from the communists. I look at Christopher. He's staring at the pictures. "Nanna. Did Grandad want to fight in Vietnam?"

"He was older and in the Army Reserves. He wanted to fight for freedom and against communism. He was excited about the adventure as well. I told him that he was too old to go. That I didn't want him to go." Nanna waits. "I was scared when he went to Vietnam, that he wouldn't come back."

"But Grandad did come home, Nanna."

"Others didn't. Grandad was lucky, but afterwards —" She stops. "Sometimes, he was very sad. It was memories of the war." Nanna shakes her head and puts her hand in front of her face. She doesn't want to talk about it.

I touch Nanna's hand before asking her, "What's in the box?"

She puts down the glass. "Grandad didn't like to talk about what was inside the box." She stammers. "Maybe it's time to show you." She holds it tightly. "Grandad's war is in here." She carefully lifts the lid.

I peer over Nanna's shoulder. In the box there are letters, a diary, black-and-white photos of mates in uniform, and medals. Nanna touches the medals. "Your grandad dragged another soldier out of the line of fire after he'd been shot. He saved his life." She takes out his medals and puts them in my hands. Tears dot the corner of her eyes.

"Grandad is a hero, Nanna."

She nods, then holds up a photo of soldiers standing in front of a Hercules plane. "There is your grandad." Nanna points to one of the soldiers. "He's wearing a slouch hat." Nanna rubs her sore fingers. "He talked to his mates who came back about what happened there. His mates were really important to him."

"What did Grandad say it was like?"

"He only told me bits and pieces." She slowly opens Grandad's diary and starts reading aloud. I think she's read this page before.

"Hard to see in the jungle. There's mud. The swamp smells. We're looking for enemy patrols. There's thirty of us. No one speaks. Want to be back at base camp. There are tents and food there. We've been eating leaves and rice gruel. My stomach's empty. There's a helicopter drop soon. Food, water. Miss home. We're on a patrol and ambush mission. Six weeks this time. Those booby traps, mines. Tom's my mate. Left his legs in the jungle. Blown off ..." Nanna closes the diary. "I don't want to read any more, Jack."

I start to hand Nanna back the medals. She shakes her head. "He'd want you to have them. They're yours now."

Goose bumps quiver down my arms and back. "I can't."

Christopher turns off the video. Nanna gets up from her armchair. "I'm tired. I'm going to rest for a little while. Your grandad wants you to have them." I follow Nanna and help her lie on her bed. Puss jumps up next to her. She turns the photo of Grandad on her side table toward her. I hold Grandad's medals tightly.

Chapter 7

What's Small, Red and Brown?

Rob's back from visiting Leo at Port. He's going to see more of him. Drive up once a month for a Rob–Leo weekend. I don't want to think about that. I show Rob Grandad's medals. Rob stands there looking at them for a long time. "They're something special, Jack."

Rob brings home a display case to put in my bedroom. "For the medals." We hang the case on my wall next to my ponto. When Mum comes in to see it, she starts crying. Then Nanna starts crying. Then Samantha cries. Rob and I just shake our heads. It's a girl disease. I feel my throat choke a little.

*　　*　　*

It's Wednesday morning and we're not going to school today. Mum's got special leave from work to take Nanna to her hospital appointment. Mum's going for her own checkup at the breast cancer screening clinic first. It's right next door. She tells Samantha, "Girls can get lumps at times. I've always had lumpy breasts."

Since I'm standing right next to Samantha, I get this exciting "lumpy breasts" news as well.

"Too much information, Mum." I scrunch my face up.

Samantha copies my scrunched-up face. "Who asked you to listen, Jack?"

Mum thinks I'm funny. I'm not being funny.

"Just don't talk about it in front of me."

Mum takes Samantha's hands and they swing their hands like a dance. "Call me Lumpy. Call me Mumpy, Lumpy-Mumpy, Lumpy-Mummy. Call me Lumpy. Call me Mumpy. That's what I am today-O." Mum's singing out of tune and Samantha is too.

"Stop," I shout.

Nanna waddles up. "Did you say 'shop,' Jack? I need some things." Then Nanna sees the dancing and begins tapping her feet. I can't help laughing. My family's crazy.

It takes a while to get everyone organized. Nanna has her handbag ready. Treats and her UNO cards. Mum's finished making sandwiches for lunch. Samantha's put in four bottles of water and some pears. We're going to have a picnic at the beach. Afterward Mum says we have to buy the wedding invitations. The wedding is only five weeks away and Mum's left the invitations really late, except the world already knows.

The waiting room at the breast-screening clinic is full. I already checked out mammograms on the Internet. It's nearly as interesting as my ponto. This special X-ray is used to take pictures of lumps and bumps inside breasts. Even men's breasts. I never knew men could have lumps there. "Hey, Samantha. Knock, knock."

"Who's there?"

"Breast."

"Breast who?"

"Breast open up and let me in!"

Samantha rolls her eyes and turns to Mum. "Do mammograms hurt, Mum?"

"Sometimes it can be a bit sore when the technician squashes your breast with a glass plate to get ready for the photos, but it's OK."

"Mum, I really, really don't want to know about this."

"But you want to be a scientist one day. You should want to understand and Samantha needs to know her body. Hormones can cause lumps every month." Mum winks at Samantha. "Even boys can get lumps."

"I know that, Mum." I didn't really know before.

Samantha sticks her tongue out at me. I pretend to catch it just as the nurse calls Mum's name. Mum insists that we go with her. We turn to Nanna, but she's fallen asleep in the chair. "She'll be all right," Mum says. We follow her and she follows the nurse, who follows the signs down a corridor with a gray vinyl floor. Mum disappears into the dressing room, then jumps out in a white sack. She swirls around. "I look like a model, don't I?"

"No, Mum."

Mum gives me her necklace to hold. "Can't wear any jewelry for the mammogram. Otherwise it'll be a picture of my necklace, not my breast."

As we tag along into the X-ray room, the technician tells us to wait outside. Mum's determined that we see what's in the room and what happens. The technician is nice and lets us go inside and see. She explains how the large metal X-ray machine works. "A plate of glass will come down. It'll press against your mum's breast, flattening it. Then the machine takes pictures."

Mum smiles at the technician. "Thank you. Now, kids, you'll have to go back out to Nanna. No one's allowed in here because X-rays send out radiation. Got to get ready to take the pictures now."

Nanna wakes up just as we arrive back in the waiting room. She holds up a pack of UNO when she sees us. "Now who's feeling lucky?" Nanna loves card games.

Mum's dressed and happy that she's had her mammogram. "That's off my list now. Nanna's results are next." We pile into the doctor's office. Goods news. Nanna only has to take pills to help her spine become stronger and exercise with her walking stick. "You will use your stick, won't you?" Mum begs Nanna as we leave the office. Nanna pretends that she will, except we all know that she won't. But I have a plan.

Lunch at the beach is good. Finding the right wedding invitation is bad. I can't stand one more shop and I'm still hungry. "Do you like these invitations, Jack? Will Rob like them? This picture of a fancy wedding is too much, don't you think?"

I don't care. I don't care. "The cards are great. Rob will like them. Anna will like them. Spot will like them. Floppy will like them. Everyone will like them." So far, every invitation has been too boring or too traditional or not right and Nanna's tired and

I'm bored and Samantha's whining. Then Mum sees a card with rainbow dream catchers and sparkles. They're not wedding invitations. Mum twiddles her fluffy hair into a ringlet. She's thinking, but it's Nanna who says, "It's your wedding. Get them if that's what makes you happy."

Samantha loves the sparkles. I love the fact Mum loves it. "Why not, Mum? It's your wedding. Just buy them."

"Jack, you're right." The relief of making a decision is major. Mum does two jumping jacks. Samantha copies her. I pound the air with my fists. Nanna's taken a cookie from her bag and has a big bite. Dream catcher wedding invitations win.

Home at last. I print out the details of the wedding on my computer — date, time, dress, address. The invitations read that Mum, Rob, Nanna, Jack, Samantha and Leo "are proud to invite you to celebrate the marriage at Sea Breeze." Samantha sticks the details inside the cards. Mum writes the names. Nanna puts them in the envelopes. Mum wants a family photo included with the invitations. She's going to get them printed. By the way, the family photo includes Leo. We're a brilliant production team, until Nanna trips on Puss. Puss squeals. Nanna squeals, but she doesn't fall over and break her leg. So it's all good.

After Nanna goes to her room for a rest before dinner, Mum gives us a guilt trip. "When I'm not here, you have to make sure that Nanna doesn't forget her walking stick." No one can make Nanna think she's old: that's why she won't use the stick. But like I said I already have a plan. A brilliant plan. I tell Mum. She thinks I'm a genius. It'll be a surprise for Nanna.

For the next two nights Samantha and I work secretly on my plan. Photos of Puss, Samantha, Mum, Rob, Grandad, Anna, the Napolis and everyone are on the floor. Samantha and I choose the best ones and arrange them into four small collages. Mum laminates them at the library. With hard-sticking wood glue, I carefully stick the collages along the stick. Nanna's so excited when we give her the walking stick that she sucks her teeth in so hard she starts choking.

Success. Nanna's family-photo walking stick is the talk of her bridge club. Now, Nanna loves using her stick. Won't go anywhere without her stick. Call me Smart Jack.

Samantha gets an A-plus for her show-and-tell mouse-house. She did help. Lucky the teacher didn't hear all the mice POOP jokes in the playground, otherwise Samantha would have gotten a D.

What's red, small and brown? Sunburned POOP.

What's brown and lights up? An electric POOP.

What are the best steps to take when you meet an escaped lion with diarrhea? Long ones.

Knock, knock.

Who's there?

Mice go.

Mice go who?

Mice go POOP, not who.

Spot, Frank, and my rat, Hector, are getting so round now that their stomachs drag along the floor. "Nanna, you have to stop giving them sweet treats." She chuckles. "It's serious, Nanna." Nanna's green eyes get greener. I just know what she's thinking. Roly-poly Nanna, roly-poly Spot, roly-poly Frank and roly-poly Hector need little treats. I start laughing. At least they'll die ecstatic.

"I'm working on our school project this afternoon at Christopher's. I'll bring you some cookies from the bakery, Nanna." I shout "bye" as I grab the book Mum borrowed on the Vietnam War. We're working on Christopher's part of the project.

Christopher lives on top of their bakery. Bread smells nearly knock me over as I walk inside. My mouth is watering and Christopher's mother hands me a sweet raisin roll. "Just baked this, Jack. It's good."

I'm stuffing the raisin roll into my mouth when Christopher's father waves us upstairs. "Go and start. Schoolwork is important." He sounds like Mum.

A few nights ago, Christopher taped an interview of his parents talking. I wasn't allowed to be there. His parents found it really hard, but they did it for Christopher. They didn't want to be filmed at all. It's just their voices on the video. I slouch on their old couch while Christopher puts on the tape. He's smart at editing anything digital. Smarter than me. The clip starts. There are flashes of Vietnam, the people, bright-green paddy fields, mountains, sandy white beaches, villages, a church, Buddhist temples. Christopher's family is Catholic. His mother's voice tells about when she was a girl playing in the stream with other children. She doesn't give any names. There are photos of kids wearing big straw hats, older people in long-sleeved caftans over loose pants. I think they're Christopher's grandparents. It makes me feel sad that they haven't got names.

Christopher's father speaks slowly. "Saigon fell to the communists. Saigon was beautiful before the war. We lived in a village near Saigon." He stops and there're tinkling sounds of Vietnamese music. The pictures keep flashing and the flutes sound like birds. Suddenly there's a crash. Drums. I jerk forward from the couch. "There were machine guns and bombs." Pictures of destroyed villages, houses, temples fill the screen. There's a photo of a screaming girl, with her clothes torn away. "Kim Phuc is the burning girl running from napalm bombs." I catch my breath. "The communists came with their flags, red with a yellow star." Christopher's father's voice becomes quieter. "Your grandparents were there. They were teachers. They hid us, but I saw the soldiers beat them. Dragging them away to prison camps. They never came back."

There's a lump in my throat.

"I never saw them again."

There's more music and then Christopher's mother's voice. "I hid too. My sister, parents and I dug a dirt hole under our house. We were there while the planes bombed us, holding each other. Afterward, there was no one left in my village." There were just war planes, burning houses, shell-shocked children and people fleeing. "There wasn't enough food." More photos. "My father said we had to leave Vietnam. Escape from our country."

The pictures on the screen change to old wooden fishing boats and high seas. "My father gave everything we had to the captain to go on the boat." Her voice is breathless. "There were so many people everywhere and there were soldiers with guns. My mother and I scrambled onto the boat, but my father and sister became separated from us in the crowds. I didn't want to leave them. I don't know where they are now." Music. "We were on the old ship for two months. The waves were big. Everyone was afraid the boat would sink. Everyone was afraid all the time. When the pirates attacked the boat, we were even more afraid. They left us water. No food, but water."

We watch the video silently. Christopher's parents say together, "We are glad that we're here with our son, Christopher."

I'm glad Christopher is here too.

He turns on the light and I look at him. My stomach's a knot. I don't feel like making a joke. Christopher nods at me. "It's OK," but it's not. How can it ever be OK? Half his family isn't here. I couldn't stand losing my family.

We take notes from the book Mum borrowed from the library.

When I leave, Christopher's parents give me a bag of sweet buns for Nanna and my family.

I'm glad to get home. Glad Nanna's asleep with her teeth falling out and Puss on her lap. Glad Mum's in the kitchen cooking. Glad Rob's in the garden trimming a tree and glad when Samantha slumps onto my bed. I take out Grandad's medals from the cabinet. Christopher's grandparents haven't got medals. I wish they had some too.

Samantha plays with Grandad's medals. I think about Christopher's other name, Peace.

Chapter 8

Sweet Buns

"Mum," I shout as I beat Samantha into the front seat of the car. Glad Mum's picking us up from school today. Samantha squeals, "It's my turn in the front seat," but I've got news. "Mum, Mum. Christopher and my Vietnam project — we're getting a prize at assembly." I look at Anna in the back seat. "Anna's Italy project is getting a prize too."

Mum starts the car, but is hardly listening. "Oh, yes. Your parents will love that, Anna."

"There're five other prizes as well. George Hamel is getting the most-improved award. Can you believe that? He did his project on England and drew a creepy plan of a ruined castle. He's not such an idiot anymore. Hey, but Christopher and I won *first* prize. We've got to do presentations for the award ceremony."

"That's lovely, Jack." Mum gives a pretend smile.

"Mum, didn't you hear me? We won first prize. There's going to be a display in the library and the school's going to write you a letter and there's going to be a morning tea."

"That's lovely," Mum says quietly again.

"Mum. Are you all right?"

"Sorry, Jack. Just thinking. It's fantastic." Mum's voice is flat like a sucked-out balloon. "Anna always does well. You and Christopher have worked so hard on the project. Grandad would have loved it." Mum catches her breath, like a sob. "That's special."

"Are you all right, Mum?" Mum gives a turn-your-lips-up smile and a pain shoots through my head. Does she miss Grandad? Is that it? Has there been an accident? Has Rob been run over? "Is Rob OK?"

"Rob? What are you talking about?"

"Is Nanna all right? She hasn't fallen over again?"

"Nanna's fine." Mum presses her fingers against her forehead. "I've got a migraine. I'm going to the doctor." She puts her hand over mine. "I'll be fine soon. I am proud of you. Proud of Christopher. And Anna too."

Mum gets migraines sometimes. As she drops us

off at home, Nanna opens the front door and Puss wanders out. I feel better when I see Nanna. She's her usual Nanna-self, wobbling, with cookie crumbs on her blouse. We wave goodbye to Mum. Anna calls her parents to tell them the news about her Italy project. There's excited shouting on the other end of the line. Anna's laughing as she puts down the phone and goes to check on Frank.

I can't believe that the wedding invitations are still piled on the hall table. They have to be mailed soon or no one will come. I'll tell Mum when she gets home. I can mail them.

Nanna beams when I announce the news about Christopher and my Vietnam project. She opens her arms. "Hug, Jack." She holds me for a long time and whispers in my ear, "Grandad hugs you too, Jack." I love Nanna and Grandad.

Samantha is busy drawing her millionth picture of a dog in her room. "I'm walking Anna home," I shout as we leave. Samantha gives us a half-wave. She's coloring in the spotty ears of a Dalmatian.

"Bye, Samantha," Anna sings out.

We walk to the beach. There are some surfers paddling out there, but there's hardly a ripple. I breathe in the salt air when the scent of something sweet wafts toward me. I turn to find out where it comes from. "Hey, Anna, you smell like peppermint."

Her curls shimmer in the sun. "Well, you better not eat me."

I grab her hand and pretend to bite it and she laughs, but then I don't let go. Her skin is soft and warm. Suddenly my heart's pounding. She doesn't pull her hand away as we walk along the beach. We only let go as we turn into the shopping street, but I still feel her fingers in the palm of my hand.

We drop into Christopher's bakery to see if he's there. He's not in the shop. Christopher's mother looks up. "Christopher's gone to the post office. He'll be back later," she explains quietly. "But I am glad you're here. I wanted to say that we're very happy about the project." She smiles. "Thank you for working with Christopher."

A shiver runs down my spine. I don't want her to thank me. It was hard for them to answer Christopher's questions. They went through so much in Vietnam. It was hard for Nanna to speak about it too. I want to tell her how brave she is, but don't know how to. I stand there on the cream tiled floor with a red face, looking like an idiot.

Anna takes over. "I didn't know much about Vietnam. It's made the class think about war and peace. About risking everything to come here. The Vietnam project is really important."

I look at Anna and know why she's so special.

Christopher's mother bends forward over the counter. "Thank you, Anna. Thank you, Jack." She picks up the metal tongs and fills two paper bags with sweet buns. "Please take them for your families."

Christopher's father appears from the back wearing his white apron. "Hello, Jack and Anna." He smiles. "We'll see you at the award ceremony."

"Yes, that'll be a great day," Anna says, as we leave.

We're nearly at Napolis' Super Delicioso Fruitologist Market when we hear Mr. Napoli's voice boom down the street. *"Bella, Anna. Bravo. Bravo. Our clever girl, è molto intelligente."* He has his arms out. Mrs. Napoli is waving her hands and there's a lot of shouting and hugging. Mr. Napoli announces that he's going to take Anna, Christopher, Samantha and me to the best ice cream shop on the beach.

I take my time walking home. Anna and I held hands. I think about that all the way back to Sea Breeze.

Rob and Mum arrive home together from work. That's strange. Mum brings home takeout Chinese food — she isn't cooking tonight. That's strange too. Mum is quiet. That's very strange.

"What did the doctor say?" I ask. She jumps. "What's wrong, Mum?"

"Nothing, Jack. Migraine."

I feel strange now. Mum has tears in her eyes. She rubs them, glances at Rob, then hurries us all to the dinner table. Nanna talks about Christopher and my Vietnam project. Rob asks a few questions, but Mum doesn't say anything.

Samantha pipes in. "I'm working on a dog project, Nanna. Do you want to see?"

How many dog projects can one girl do? She races

to her room and comes back with a pile of pictures for a poster. By now dinner's over and Rob heads for the kitchen sink. He nudges me. "Why don't you help your sister with her poster? I don't need dish-washing help tonight." I start to object, but I can see Rob wants to do it alone today. I wander over to Samantha to check out her drawings. I sneak a look at Mum and Rob. They are whispering and acting differently. I get this scared feeling.

"When everyone's ready, I'd like a family talk tonight." Mum takes lemonade and the sweet buns Christopher's parents gave us to the family room.

I give Mum a question-mark look. What's all the weirdness about? Leo pops into my mind and that shooting pain charges through my head. If Leo is going to live here, that's bad. There's not enough room. He can visit, but this is my house. Rob walks into the family room and brings up Leo. My stomach sinks, but then he says, "Since Leo surfed here, he's joined his local Surf Lifesaving Club. He's liking it more up north."

So it's not about Leo. Maybe this is just another wedding talk. I can't take any more wedding plans. Those invitations *have* to be mailed now. They're piled next to the mice, being splattered with mouse poop. Nanna's comfy in her armchair with Puss on her lap. Samantha is on the couch. Rob stands with his feet apart and rubs his head. We're waiting. Mum's next to him. We're waiting. Samantha leans over to Nanna and pats Puss. We're waiting. Can Mum hurry up? I have to check my ponto. Write up scientific notes. Then I want to go through my photos of Anna and find a good one. Rob clears his throat. "The wedding."

I'm right. It's about the wedding. Groan.

"Rob and I are getting married and everything's going ahead. It's just —" Mum stops.

Rob puts his hand over Mum's. "The wedding will be later. Not next month. Just a bit later."

I don't understand and look at Nanna and then Samantha.

"But my peach dress. Anna's peach dress. We have our dresses."

"You will wear them, darling." Mum walks over to Samantha and sits next to her. "There's still going to be a wonderful wedding. It's just going to be later."

"I don't understand," Samantha whispers.

I don't either. We've been doing nothing but talking about and organizing the wedding. Why would they change the date? This doesn't make sense. Rob's going to be my stepdad. Suddenly a bad feeling grips me. Is he going to live with Leo? But Rob and Mum are getting married. Unless … I stare at Rob, then Mum. What else could it be? I stumble over the question. "Rob, are you leaving us?"

Rob jerks forward with surprise on his face. "No, Jack. I'd never leave your mum and you kids." He looks at Nanna. "Or Nanna."

Nanna's voice wobbles. "Please tell us what's wrong."

Mum presses her lips together. "I'm going to be all right." She shuffles back onto the couch. "I am all right. The tests show I have —" Mum puts her arms around Samantha. "We can work it out." She slips out the words. "It's breast cancer."

We're looking at Mum. I don't know what she means.

"It's all right. I'll be all right … good doctors … the mammogram … caught early … best treatment …" I'm trying to figure out what she's saying, but her words jump all over the place. Breast cancer? Suddenly my head is spinning, my gut shrivels. I don't get it. *Cancer?* What's Mum talking about? She said she had a migraine. That's what she said. That's why she went to the doctor. Mum's got a migraine.

"Breast cancer has good treatments." Stop talking, Mum. Stop talking. Samantha's crying. Mum's hugging her. Samantha's sobbing now. The whole room fills with Samantha's sobs. I look at Mum's face and she's crying too. Mum's a liar, a liar. She has a migraine. There's a wedding. Leo's a penguin. Nanna's got a walking stick. Christopher and I won a prize, my ponto … Suddenly the sky is crashing down. I bend over and press my face into my hands.

I don't know when Rob sat next to me, but he's rubbing my back and talking. "We're a family. We'll figure this out, Jack."

I look up at him. It's hard to speak. "But it's cancer, Rob." I can't live without Mum. None of us can live without Mum.

Chapter 9

Red Eyes

I hear Nanna pad into the bathroom. I can't sleep. Hector keeps me company. He doesn't sleep much at night. I scratch his ears. He likes that and chatters his teeth. Hector needs another rat friend in his cage because he gets lonely when I'm not around. I have to persuade Mum. I catch my breath. I can't ask Mum now. I notice light streaking under my door. It opens and Samantha's head appears. "Jack. Are you awake?"

"Sure I'm awake. Come and pat Hector."

Samantha walks toward me, holding Floppy. As she strokes Hector, I see that her eyes are red. Hector has red eyes too. Normally I'd make a joke, but I can't now. "Can I stay here?" Samantha's scared

to sleep alone tonight. She sits cross-legged on my bed, hugging Floppy.

"Hey, everything is going to be fine."

"What if Mum …?" Samantha starts sobbing again and I put my arms around her. I gulp hard. I refuse to cry.

"Mum will be all right. She always is." I lie like Mum lied. I don't know what's going to happen, except I have to make Samantha feel better.

I talk for a while about the wedding. "Mum and Rob are going to get married. You and Anna are going to be great flower girls. It'll just be later." Samantha smiles for the first time tonight. I tell her about my new experiments and talk and talk until her eyelids slowly shut. She falls asleep with Floppy beside her.

I lie on my back thinking. Anna and I held hands at the beach. It was special, but it feels like a long time ago. Working on the Vietnam project with Christopher was incredible. I wanted the prize, but I don't want it now. I'd swap it in a second for Mum not to be sick. I close my eyes and half-sleep, but suddenly I'm awake. I sleep, then wake up, sleep, then wake up. Time is going so slowly. I look at my watch. Two in the morning. Mum's going back to the breast cancer clinic with Rob. I want to go with her, but Mum said that I have to take care of Samantha and Nanna at home. We're allowed to miss school today. I couldn't face school. I'm not allowed to tell anybody about this, except Anna.

I close my eyes. Suddenly I can't breathe. I'm trying to get air, but it won't come into my lungs. I don't know what's happening. I put my hands over my face. It's wet. I wipe my face, but it gets wetter and wetter.

Three in the morning. I'm on the computer looking up breast cancer. It's pretty common. I don't want it to be common. I don't want Mum to have it. Cells go crazy and keep dividing until they become a lump or tumor and take over your body. The main thing is to catch the cancer early. I just want Mum to have caught it early. Get rid of it and then be back to normal. That's what I want. She has to beat it. I'm so tired. I can't think anymore. I turn the computer off. I hear Nanna pad into the bathroom again.

Four o'clock, I get an orange juice from the kitchen. I notice that the pile of wedding invitations isn't on the hall table anymore. My stomach sinks.

Five in the morning: I watch Samantha sleeping and Hector snoozing.

Six in the morning: I hear Nanna pad to the bathroom. She really has a weak bladder. I'm getting up. This is the longest night ever.

Seven in the morning: I call Anna. "Won't be at school today."

"Jack, are you there?" I try to speak. "Are you there?" Anna repeats the question until I force out a reply.

"Yes." My voice cracks.

"What's wrong, Jack?"

I press my hand against my head, blocking out the shooting pains. "You can't tell anyone."

"I won't. I promise."

"It's. Mum." I can't breathe and I bend over winded, gasping for air.

Anna's voice is urgent. "What's happened? What is it? Just tell me. Tell me."

Coughing, I splutter a huge sob through the phone. "Mum has breast cancer." I don't wait for Anna's answer. I race down the back steps into the garden, and stand panting beside the sunflowers where Patch is buried. I hide my head in my arms. I don't care if Leo lives with us. I don't care if Mum calls me darling or does jumping jacks or makes me wear a penguin suit. She can do all of that. I don't care about any of it. Mum has to be OK. She just has to be. Everything crashes in my head, and the tears spill down my face and I know I'm crying. I'm crying until my body hurts and my throat is sore and my eyes are red.

We wave goodbye to Mum and Rob as they drive off to the hospital. It's going to be a long wait for them to come home. Nanna has her walking stick in her hand and is wearing her favorite cardigan. "We're visiting Grandad today. Samantha, can you pack a morning snack? Jack, you get a brush and garden scissors to trim Grandad's grave, and get some sunflowers too."

"Grandad will love the sunflowers." Samantha doesn't smile.

"We need to talk to him."

It's a relief to be doing something. Samantha puts water, fruit and cookies and a picnic blanket inside a backpack. She straps Floppy on the top of it. I get the garden tools from the shed, then cut three sunflowers. I put on the backpack. Samantha holds the sunflowers and we head for the bus stop.

Nanna shuffles into the bus seat reserved for people with walking sticks. I sit beside her and Samantha sits hugging Floppy at the window. The window is open because she gets bus-sick sometimes.

"I can always depend on you, Jack." Nanna brushes the photos on her walking stick with the soft pads of her fingertips. "You're such a wonderful boy. I heard you last night with Samantha."

I don't feel wonderful. What else could I do? Nanna doesn't fall asleep on the bus ride like she usually does. The bus stops at the cemetery gates and Nanna steps off without tripping. We head toward Grandad. The sun is amber; the sea is frothed with creamy butter; and the skies are wavy. It's like Grandad is here: it feels safe. I snip the grass that has grown around his grave while Samantha puts the sunflowers beside the headstone.

We settle onto the blanket, take out our snack, and look at Grandad's grave and past it all the way to the fishing boats bobbing in the sea. I take photos of the sky, sea, clouds and Samantha lying, her head on Floppy. "Jack's photos are very special," she tells Grandad. I click a few pictures of Nanna.

She's an amazing subject. She tells Grandad about the Vietnam project and Christopher and our award. Her green eyes fill with tears. "I am so proud of them. I know you are too."

"Anna got a prize as well," Samantha whispers.

I tell Grandad how much his medals hanging in my bedroom mean to me. Nanna nods, making gentle sucking sounds with her teeth. We talk about Christopher's parents and their bakery, Nanna's bargains, George Hamel who isn't a bully anymore and cookies that stick in Nanna's teeth. Nanna flashes her "renovated" new teeth and it feels so good to smile.

Samantha fiddles with the fringe of the blanket. "Mum and Rob's wedding is going to be later, Grandad."

"Samantha, the wedding will be beautiful and you will be too." Nanna taps her feet. "And we'll dance."

The water tastes good. Nanna eats a banana. I take a breath and finally ask Grandad, "Mum is sick. What are we supposed to do?"

Nanna walks to the side of Grandad's grave. She puts her hand on his headstone. I copy her. The stone feels warm. "Life is going to be different for a while."

"I don't want it to be different." Samantha stands between us.

"It will be, Samantha. Sometimes Mum's going to be tired and sick. Sometimes she won't be there just when you want to talk to her. You might even think she doesn't love you then. That's never true."

"I'm scared." Samantha leans against Nanna.

"Don't be scared. You have to find the times when she is feeling better, when she can hear you and you can laugh and talk. This is your mum's time to work hard so she can win against cancer. You can be there for her by being the great kids you are now. Doing a project on Vietnam with Christopher, Jack, or one on dogs, Samantha. Going to school, taking photos, baking a terrific cake, changing the light bulbs, surfing, putting beads in your hair. All the things you do."

"That doesn't help Mum."

"It does, Jack. She'll know you are all right, so she doesn't have to worry." Nanna looks at Samantha seriously. "It's brave to get dressed for school, do your schoolwork and play handball with your friends when Mum is sick and you can't talk to them about it. When the other children don't understand that Mum mightn't feel up to making dinner one night or she's quiet and you're worried. Can you be brave?"

"I don't know," Samantha whispers.

I nod. "If we are here for each other, we'll be here for Mum."

*   *   *

School's finished for the day. "Jack, Jack." I look out of my window. Anna is puffing as she runs up the back stairs of the house. She races inside with her arms pounding, hair flying and her eyes red.

Chapter 10

Should We Tell?

Rob's car swerves into the driveway just after Anna goes home. I jump down the steps in one go, with Samantha racing after me. I shout, "Mum, Mum, what happened?"

Mum jerks her head forward, as if she hasn't seen me. "Later, Jack. Please." Mum's voice is really quiet. "Just need a little time to myself."

"But Mum, what's the doctor said?"

"Please, Jack. Not now." Mum turns her back on me, then speaks to Samantha. "I'll talk to you soon, Samantha."

"But Mum —"

"Not now, Jack."

"You heard her, Jack. Give Mum a chance to unwind."

I stand there as Mum disappears into her bedroom. She doesn't care. Samantha runs into her room. Nanna goes with Rob into the kitchen to make coffee. They're talking, but we're not invited. My throat knots like a stuck video clip. We've been waiting all day for Mum to come home. All day we've waited, but Samantha and I don't matter. I plod down the hall, knock on Samantha's door. A wispy gulp answers, "Come in." Samantha's lying on her ballerina blanket with her face buried in Floppy. She looks up. Her face is blotchy and streaked with crying. I sit next to her.

"Dinner." Rob opens Samantha's bedroom door. I'm not talking to him. He holds out his hand for Samantha. She takes it.

It's the corner-shop roast chicken tonight. Nanna pats my chair. "Come and sit next to me, Jack." I slouch beside her.

Mum clears her throat. "Sorry I couldn't speak to you when I got home." I roll the peas on my plate with my fork. "Jack, are you all right?" No, I'm not. How can I be? I'm not talking to you, Mum. "Jack. I need you." I squash three peas into mash. Mum puts her hand over Samantha's. "I need you too. I want to explain what's happened and what's happening. Jack, do you want to know?" I shrug.

"When I had the mammogram, the radiologist saw an abnormal area. I had an ultrasound afterward. A lady put gel on my breast and took computer pictures with sound waves. Made it easier to see what was in my breast. You would have been interested, Jack."

I am interested. My stomach knots, and I just shrug again.

"Then the doctor did a biopsy. This time he used the ultrasound to find the lump to see where he had to put the needle, to take out some cells."

"Did it hurt?" Samantha hugs Mum.

Mum gives a crooked smile. "Not too much, but I didn't like it."

I want to hug Mum too. "The lump is in my right breast. The surgeon is going to cut out the cancer. Maybe he'll cut out some of the lymph nodes in my armpit too if there are cancer cells there."

"Will it hurt?" Samantha's ponytail bobs up and down as she presses even closer to Mum.

"I don't know, Samantha."

I feel rotten. I don't want Mum to have surgery. What if something happens to her?

Rob throws me a look. "Come on, Jack. You always have questions."

Mum's eyes are watering. What am I doing? I don't want Mum to cry. I love her and I do have questions. I push the peas on my plate to the side. "Mum, what are lymph nodes?"

Rob winks at me, Nanna smiles and I feel a bit better.

Mum looks up for a minute to get her thoughts organized. Mum isn't a scientist like me and needs time to figure it out. "Lymph glands. They protect you against infection. Cancer cells want to get into the lymph glands so they can go to other places in you. The surgery cuts out the cancer in my breast and maybe under my arm."

"So when's the operation, Mum?"

"Next week, Jack," Mum adds quickly.

My stomach drops. It's so soon.

"And I'm going to get through it fine. I'll only be in the hospital for a few days. Then there are other treatments like radiation therapy, and maybe chemotherapy. I'll tell you when I know more about them." Mum looks at my dinner plate and teases me. "You've made a mess of your peas."

"Jack doesn't like peas," Samantha whispers.

I ignore Samantha, but I make a deal in my head. I'll eat peas every dinner, every day, all the time, if Mum gets better.

Samantha tells Mum and Rob that we visited Grandad's grave. "We went on the bus and I didn't get bus-sick."

Nanna closes her eyes for a minute like she's there. "It was a lovely morning. We told Grandad everything and we put sunflowers on the grave. Jack took some photos."

"Sunflowers." Mum sighs. "I'd love to see the pictures."

"All right, Mum." I walk to my room. Don't feel like running today. I bring back my camera and show everyone the shots. I'll edit them later. I stop at the photo of Nanna waving her walking stick over the grave.

"Grandad liked the walking stick with the photos." Nanna's face crinkles into a grin. She lifts her walking stick up, even though we've seen it lots of times. Samantha points to the photo of Grandad. Mum smiles and that feels good.

"It's going to be hard sometimes, but I am going to be all right." Mum looks at Samantha and me. "But you have to help me. I'm going to get tired. I need to know that you're going to be all right even if I can't spend as much time taking care of you as I always want to."

"OK, Mum."

Rob makes coffee for Nanna and Mum.

I ask, "Is this going to be a secret, Mum?" It's so hard to keep it a secret. "Everyone will want to know why the wedding's later. Why you're not at work or college …" My questions dribble to a stop.

"I had to tell work. Rob told his work too." Mum presses her fingers against her lips. "I don't want a lot of phone calls and visits. I love my friends, but they'll be exhausting."

"Anna's trying not to tell her parents. She hates hiding things from them."

"The Napolis are good friends." Mum sips her coffee. "It's not fair to put Anna under that stress. They should know."

Rob has to tell Leo. Nanna can't keep a secret for long, so it'll get out. School needs to know. Friends will be hurt if we don't tell them. Christopher's parents are making the wedding cake. They should know. Rob finally asks Mum, "What do you want us to do?"

Mum rests her head in the palms of her hands. When she lifts her head, she looks different. "I don't want lies. You can share this with whomever you feel you want to, but please ask them not to phone too much. Send me a note, write a card, send love. That's what I'd like."

Rob's on the phone. "Sounds like the surf is great, Leo … Love to see you in the competition next week, but something's happened … Breast cancer … I can't come up for a while … The wedding's postponed … Hope you understand —"

Leo's scared. He wants his dad.

I'm on the phone. "Anna, you can tell your parents … Mum doesn't want you to hide it anymore … Surgery's next week … She's going to be all right … It's caught early … See you at school tomorrow."

Anna's scared. Parents can get very sick.

I'm on the phone. "Mum's coming to the award ceremony, Christopher … Breast cancer … Mum asked if your parents could make the wedding cake for later … See you at school tomorrow."

Christopher's scared. He knows about losing family.

Nanna's scared. She wants Grandad here because Mum's sick.

Rob's scared. Nothing's going to work if Mum isn't here.

Samantha and I are scared. Mum has to make it.

Everything's going so fast. Mum has a meeting with the principal. Mr. Angelou tells me that I can talk to him anytime I need to.

Christopher and I have to complete our presentation on our Vietnam project for the award ceremony. "It'll make your mum proud, Jack," Mr. Angelou says. I don't feel like doing it, but I can't let Christopher down, or Mr. Angelou and especially not Mum.

The Napolis send a gigantic basket filled with mangoes, green apples, melons and red grapes. Christopher's parents send a gigantic basket of breads and pastries, with cookies, sweet buns and flaky cheese swirls.

The wedding plans have been postponed for a date unknown. Rob says he is already my stepdad. "Nothing's changed," he says. But it has. Leo sends a get-well card to Mum, a spotty place mat with a photo of a Dalmatian to Samantha and a joke to me:

The police are looking for a cane toad with one eye called Wally.

What's his other eye called?

I take Wally down from the top of the cupboard. He's only got one eye. It's not a very good joke, but Leo's OK. I send him a photo of my ponto and a surfing poster.

Anna and I haven't had time to walk along the beach again. I wonder if she still likes me.

Award ceremony at school.

Mr. Napoli arrives in a navy-blue suit, light-blue shirt and multicolored tie. His hair is slicked back and his moustache trimmed and neat. Mrs. Napoli is wearing an orange dress and black high heels. I've never seen them look so dressed-up. I click photos.

Christopher's mother is wearing a sapphire-blue áo-dài — a tunic — over long flowing pants. There are glass diamonds sparkling from her sleeves. His father is wearing a gray Mandarin jacket over loose white pants. I click photos.

Mum is like sunflowers at Sea Breeze with a yellow ribbon hairband holding back her blond hair. Her spring dress is printed with daisy rings. Rob is wearing his green-checked shirt and blue jeans and I want to burst into a trucking song. I click photos.

Mr. Angelou welcomes parents, teachers, students and visitors, then launches into his speech about the project. "The students have produced a special exhibition of countries. Please take your time to enjoy the displays by the class after the awards. This is a celebration of the many cultures that make up

this school community." His bald head beams in the hall light. "Six students have produced exceptional work. I am very proud to welcome the award-winners onto the stage." Everyone climbs up and sits in the seats behind the lectern.

The presentations on Afghanistan, Sudan and Israel are really interesting. George Hamel is quick with a PowerPoint slide show of illustrations and pictures of the castle. It's Anna's turn. She walks to the lectern with her notes, and I can only see her profile with her dark hair bouncing. Photos of vineyards and olive groves, the stone farmhouse with her grandparents looking really young, the cliffs plunging into the Mediterranean Sea, the family kitchen filled with glass bottles and tomatoes cooking, move across the screen. Anna ends with a photo of a ship leaving Italy.

"It was a big move for my parents to leave Italy and their families and friends, but they found new families and friends here. They speak English today, as well as Italian. My parents have their own Fruitologist Market and this is the Napoli home now."

Everyone cheers for Anna, especially Mr. and Mrs. Napoli. Then it is Christopher and my turn. I am nervous even though we spent a lot of time preparing this. Most of it is the film clip and slideshow. Grandad's medals, Christopher's parents' voices, scenes from the Vietnam War, fishing boats that faced pirates and the high seas, soldiers, homeless families, camps, bombed land and that photo of the girl Kim Phuc running from the napalm bombs as her village burned and she burned.

Christopher and I look at each other for the final part of the presentation. This is the script we read out.

Jack: "My grandad …"

Christopher: "My grandfather …"

Jack and Christopher together: "… were in the Vietnam War."

Jack: "My family …"

Christopher: "My family …"

Jack and Christopher together: "… are friends today in a new country."

Jack and Christopher together: "Kim Phuc, the girl running from the bomb, said, 'Don't see a little girl crying out in fear and pain. See her as crying out for peace.'"

Christopher's mother has tears in her eyes. Mum does too.

Mum is having surgery tomorrow.

Chapter 11

The Surgery

"Aren't you hungry?" I ask Mum. She's not allowed to eat or drink anything this morning.

Her bag is at the front door. Mum's packed the pajamas we bought her from Susie's Super Discount Store. Nanna's favorite shop. They're bright-pink with white woolly sheep and stars all over them. Mum loves the pink flowers in the sheep's hair. Nanna loves the pajamas too. Samantha and I secretly bought a Nanna-size pair for her birthday. Rob's got a day off work to take Mum to the hospital. We're staying home to be with Nanna.

"I'm going to be fine, everyone," Mum says as she hugs us.

Rob carries her bag to the car. "I'll phone as soon as Mum's out of surgery."

We wave as Mum and Rob drive away.

Nanna wobbles into her armchair. Puss curls into her lap. Samantha sits next to Nanna, patting Puss. They look like misery-guts. I don't feel really good either, but we can't sit there all day. Mum wouldn't want that.

"Come on. We've got stuff to do." Nanna, Samantha and Puss look up. "Don't you want to make Mum happy?" Nanna rubs her eyes. Samantha nods. Puss purrs.

The kitchen table is cleared. Glue, ribbons, cardboard, sparkles, colored pencils, scissors. Samantha is in charge of the card-making with Nanna and Puss as helpers. I head for the workshop. I've got an idea.

The workshop looks good. Everything's in the right place. I use Leo's workbench to set up. He won't mind. Not here anyway. Wood, glue, saw, paintbrush, paint, paper and pencil to draw the design. I start.

"Lunch, Jack," Samantha calls from the back door. Can't believe the time. It's already after one o'clock. I race up the back stairs. I'm starving. Nanna's made strawberry jam sandwiches and there's a bowl of bananas. Her favorite. Samantha's jumping around showing me their card. "It's fantastic." There's a dog on it of course. It's a party card with so many sparkles, glitter, colors and "GET WELL QUICK" written in gold.

"What have you made, Jack?" Nanna says, chewing her banana.

"You'll see when I'm finished." I bite into my strawberry jam sandwich. Suddenly, the phone rings. I grab it, spitting jam everywhere. "It's Rob, Rob." Coughing, I splutter, "Mum's out of surgery." I yell, "She's all right. All right."

Samantha starts crying. Nanna smiles like the Cheshire Cat and Puss purrs and purrs and purrs.

It's been one day since the operation. Finally Rob is taking Samantha and me to visit Mum in the hospital. Samantha is holding the special Mum party card. I'm carrying the present I made.

"Just take it easy when you see Mum." Rob puts his arm on my shoulder.

Why is Rob saying that? Mum's all right, isn't she? We go into her ward. There's Mum in the bed next to the window. I spot the bright-pink pajamas and the sheep. We race toward her. Mum smiles and my stomach sinks. She looks sick. There are bandages over her chest. She's got a needle in her hand attached to an IV.

"She's been vomiting from the anesthetic," Rob says.

It hurts her to move. Mum hides a groan as she sits up to look at Samantha's card. "It's beautiful, darling." Samantha smiles because she likes to be called darling. I don't. Mum reaches for my present. "You're so clever, Jack, making this." It was not that hard to make. I did a tech drawing first, then sawed the wood into a heart shape. The middle part was the hardest, where I slotted in the photo of Samantha and me. There's a stand that I glued to the back of the heart frame. "I love it, Jack." I put it on the cabinet next to her bed. Mum keeps looking at it.

Mum's been in the hospital for two days. Nanna, Samantha and I have been cooking. I made eggs for dinner one night. It was a great success. Nanna cooked a roast lamb one night that was good too. Mrs. Napoli sent us a huge bowl of pasta and Christopher's parents sent over two loaves of fresh bread. I'm washing the dishes because Rob goes to the hospital every night to be with Mum. We're trying to keep the house clean, but it's hard. Rob says that Mum'll be home soon.

After school, Anna and I walk along the beach. "So glad your mum is getting better."

Small ripples of relief spread over me. "She's made it through the first part. She's still sore, but the IV is out now. She's got radiation therapy, and maybe chemotherapy, but Mum'll be home soon. I just want Mum to get better and not have cancer." Anna hugs me for a second and it feels good. We walk between the rocks. The air smells like seaweed. The waves rush in, then get sucked out. I climb up a boulder and reach out for Anna's hand to help her up. We sit looking out to sea holding hands.

It's Saturday morning and Mum's coming home today. We're all so excited. I clean the mouse-house. I hate doing that, but I didn't want the hallway to smell of mouse poop. Mum likes Frank and Spot better than she used to, but she's still not a mouse person.

The house is like a garden. Flowers everywhere. The library, Rob's work, Mr. Angelou — lots of people have sent flowers. Samantha and Nanna are in charge of flower arrangements. "We need more vases." Nanna fiddles with the red and white roses. She's bending to smell the scent when *pop*. I can't believe it. Samantha yelps, "Yuk," but Nanna just laughs a toothless laugh.

"Nanna, your teeth." She pops them back in and twinkles a toothy smile. I groan as I race to the kitchen cupboard. Found it. I produce Mum's big glass jug. "A vase."

"You are clever, Jack." There are some plastic jugs as well. I find some garden pots from the workshop; we have plenty of vases and Samantha and Nanna are happy as pigs in mud. Hey, I feel funny again. Pig joke, pig joke.

"Nanna, Nanna. Why is getting up at five in the morning like a pig's tail?"

"Why, Jack?"

"Because it's twirly. Get it? Too early?"

Nanna laughs and laughs. Samantha complains. "Jack, that is a stupid joke."

"Oink, oink, oink." I pull Samantha's pigtails.

"Don't, Jack!" But she's laughing. We're all happy that Mum's coming home.

Anna arrives with a wheely bag filled with fruit and vegetables. She's brought them all the way from Napolis' Super Delicioso Fruitologist Market. Her face is flushed. I try not to look at her because I don't want to get red too. Nanna hugs Anna for ages.

The fridge is now full of the Napolis' fruit and vegetables. Christopher dropped off some bread and six cookies last night. I notice that there are only two cookies left and Samantha and I didn't eat any. "Who ate them?" I stare directly at Nanna. She gives a guilty giggle.

Anna and Samantha start making a banana cake — Mum's favorite. Mine too. I get my hammer and tacks from the workshop to hang the "Welcome Home" banner in the family room. Samantha has drawn a dog on the banner, of course.

Lunchtime. Everything is done. Anna stays. We're hanging around waiting. Nanna brews a cup of tea. I squeeze oranges and make six glasses of juice. I check the thermometer. The weather's just right. Puss is purring. Nanna brings out her cards. Samantha's sticking her head out of the window. Suddenly Samantha squeals, "Car coming, car coming."

There's a hand waving from the passenger-side window. It's Mum's, and we all pile out into the driveway, waving back. "Hold on," Rob yells. He stops the car, then gets out to open Mum's door for her. She hobbles onto the path in her pink hibiscus dressing-gown. Matches her pajamas.

"Mum, are you going to do some jumping jacks?"

"Very funny, Jack."

"We've baked you a banana cake." Samantha bounces around. "Anna brought the bananas." Anna gives a huge smile.

"But Nanna ate the cookies."

"Cookies? Samantha, did you say cookies?" Nanna's hearing is bad today. "They were delicious." That makes us all laugh, which makes Nanna laugh.

Slowly Mum walks up the steps into Sea Breeze. She notices right away that the mouse-house is clean. She's happy about that. She walks down the hallway toward the family room and smiles at the sunflowers on the hall table. But when she enters the family room, she stops still. Roses and jasmine and daffodils and lilies and my banner fill the room. She starts crying and can't stop. "Don't cry, Mum. Don't cry, Mum." Samantha tries to hug her, but Rob puts an arm around each of us kids. "Mum's still a bit sore today."

"This is so beautiful." Mum swallows tears. "I'm so happy to see you and to be home. This is the best homecoming I could ever imagine."

No work for Mum for a while. She's not allowed to lift anything heavy for ages. It's our job to buy the week's groceries, do the laundry, gardening, cooking and everything. Mum says it's like being on vacation. If you ask me, it's not much of a vacation with a cut down your chest. Mum always sees the positive side of things.

I head off to do late-night shopping with Rob and Samantha. Nanna's coming too. She wants to buy more underpants. Hers have little fur-balls on them from too many washes. She's decided to buy us some more too. How many underpants does a kid need? Please, please can all the purple ones be sold out?

We head for the supermarket. Nanna says she wants to look around and will catch us at the doughnut cafe afterward. What a surprise. Doughnuts are a huge Nanna favorite. Samantha is super-annoying when she won't move from the hair aisle. She needs shampoo and conditioner and sparkles and ribbons. She's going to be a hairdresser for sure. Mum's written us a list of what we really have to get — meat, vegetables, drinks, milk, eggs, the usual. Oh, I see some wood glue. There's a hardware part in the cleaning aisle. "Rob, can I …?"

Before I even finish he nods at me. "Throw it into the cart."

Rob pays at the checkout and I push the cart toward the doughnut cafe. I see Nanna at a table with parcels. She's beaming as she waves her walking stick at us. I'm suspicious. "Sit down, sit down." We order doughnuts and strawberry smoothies, and then Nanna announces her success. "Look what I've got!" She rummages in a shopping bag, then flaunts them. You guessed it. They're purple and big and the last ones in the shop. How lucky am I? *NOT.*

I can't believe it's been two weeks already. Mr. Angelou has been especially nice to me and I didn't get into trouble for accidentally hitting the handball into the street. Christopher let me win at handball and I walked with Anna to the rocks again. I really like Anna and I think she likes me. The flowers are gone from the family room and I took down the banner. Mum's back at the library part time, but her arm hurts her. I don't know if she'll ever be able to do jumping jacks again. I worry.

I'm checking out my ponto when I hear Mum arrive home. I race out right away with my ponto. "Look how enormous it is and —" I stop. She has purple marks on her chest. "What's that, Mum?"

"It's nothing." It *is* something.

"What's that, Mum?" I ask again.

Mum rubs her forehead, then quickly looks at me. "The doctor marked my chest, that's all. It's planning for the radiation therapy. Can we talk about it later? I need to lie down, darling."

That's all? It's not all and I'm not her *darling*. I follow Mum down the hallway. Mum turns around, then kisses my cheek. "Just need a little rest, darling." She shuts the bedroom door.

I stand there for a while, check Frank and Spot in the hallway, then flop onto my bed. I put my ponto on my windowsill near Hector. I open his cage and pat him, trying to figure out what the purple really means. I have an idea. I head for my computer. "Purple and radiation therapy." There's lots of information. "The area to be treated will be marked with a pink/purple marker and/or permanent tattoos ... The tattoos are small pinprick-size black/purple marks, tattooed on the skin." Has Mum got tattoos? I can't believe that. I keep reading. Radiation therapy is X-rays that blast cancer cells, but it doesn't hurt. Except Mum's going to be tired. Her skin's going to be red and sore. She has to go every day for weeks and weeks. A scared feeling burbles inside me.

Mum's cooked sausages and steak for dinner. Nanna likes the sausages because they don't stick in her teeth. Mum's put Samantha's card on the fridge and my heart photo frame on the shelf. "They're beautiful," Mum says for the hundredth time. "Jack, do you have any jokes?" I shake my head. I don't feel like joking.

Rob brings up the radiation. "Mum's starting in a few weeks' time."

Suddenly Samantha spots it. "There's purple on you, Mum."

"Ask Mum to show you her purple tattoos." I give Mum the look, that I know she's hiding them.

Samantha pipes up, "Don't be dumb, Jack. Mum hasn't got tattoos."

"That's me, the tattooed lady. I wanted them to tattoo your names on my breast, but they wouldn't."

"Can I see?" Samantha's wagging her ponytail like a puppy dog's tail. I'm really un-funny tonight. Not in the mood.

"I don't like tattoos." Nanna's face creases into a wrinkle.

Mum's laughing as she shows us two tiny dots. "I don't think I'd be a great attraction at the circus with this."

We're all laughing now, until Rob ruins everything. "I want to see Leo before Mum starts radiation."

I'm not interested. I shove my chair back. "I've got to check out my ponto and fungus."

"Hold on, Jack. I'm driving up to see Leo this weekend." As if I care. "There's a great fishing spot in the National Park. Great place to camp." As if I care. "Thought we'd drive up together. We can have a boys' weekend. What do you think?"

I just stand there like a stunned fish head. Rotten joke. Mouth open, feeling like an idiot.

"What about me? I want to go too."

"Samantha, we can have a special girls' weekend. Just Nanna, you, me."

"And Anna?" Samantha pipes in.

"Yes, Anna too. We'll go to the markets, have a sundae at the ice cream shop." Nanna's happy because she loves sundaes and going out.

I really want to go camping with Rob, but maybe I shouldn't go. What if Mum needs me? What if Nanna falls? Samantha always needs me to do something too. But I want to go with Rob. He asked me, like he's my dad. Not that he is or anything, but he wants us to drive up together. Just us.

Rob reads my mind. "Mum will be fine. The Napolis are dropping by and she's better anyway."

Is Mum really better? "OK, Rob. I'll come."

"Then you'd better pack your fishing gear. We're going tomorrow."

Nanna's face shines. "It was Grandad's fishing gear. It's Jack's now. You've made Grandad happy, Jack."

The four-wheel drive is loaded. We strap the tents onto the roof-racks. Sleeping bags, folding table and three chairs, camp stove, lamp, fishing rods, food and water. Everything fits in and we're heading north.

Rob's seen some weird and funny license plates in Spare Parts. "What do you think of these, Jack?"

IXELR8 — I accelerate (that's so smart).

2KUL4U — Too cool for you (even smarter).

LV2EAT — Love to eat (Mum wants that one).

2phast — Too fast (ME).

IDIOT (who'd want that?).

NERD (that's worse).

We listen to music for a while, eat, drink, talk about cars. "Did you hear about that guy in America who built a pickup truck from spare parts? Heaps of colors and even though it looks weird, it works."

"That's impressive, but what sort of car do you want?"

"I'm going to do up a secondhand van and put on mag wheels, speakers at the back …" I go on for ages. Rob talks about what parts I can use to get precision tuning and I start to relax. We drive along the freeway for a while, then onto main roads along the coast. The CD's humming when I take a breath. I have to ask Rob. "Is Mum going to be all right, Rob? Don't just say she's fine. I need to know."

Rob glances at me, doesn't answer at first. He drives for a while. "OK, Jack. Mum will be fine, but there's still a way to go." He takes his time. "Radiation therapy is for around six weeks and Mum'll go in every day except weekends. She gets the radiation where the cancer was removed. It won't hurt, but she'll be tired and it will be like her chest is really sunburned."

"And will it come back?" My stomach knots.

"The pills help prevent that. The surgery and radiation prevent that too. But no one's a hundred percent sure." The knot in my stomach gets harder. "Some people have chemotherapy as well, but Mum's not. Chemo kills cancer cells."

"Why won't Mum be having that?"

"Her cancer was caught early enough. She didn't have cancer cells spreading under her arm and that's great news."

"Great news," I repeat Rob. Is it?

"The cancer in her breast was just an inch in diameter and the surgeon cut away a lot around it. If Mum had chemo, it'd mean months of treatment and side effects. She'd feel pretty sick too."

I don't want Mum to be sick. I feel sick.

"The doctor said that as long as she takes special hormone pills it would be all right." Rob puts his hand on my shoulder. "It's Mum's choice, Jack. I believe she'll be fine."

"Do you, Rob?" I stammer.

"Yes, I do."

Leo's waiting for us at the front of his apartment. He races into the car, waves to his mother and we're off to the National Park. We want to set up camp while there's light. "We're going to have a great time, boys, and we'll be eating fish tomorrow night. Fish we catch."

Leo taps Rob on his shoulder. "Dad, thanks for coming."

"I'll always come for you, Leo." He looks at me sideways. "And for you, Jack."

"I'm sorry about your mum, Jack." I can see that he really means it.

I don't mind Leo in the front seat. I sat next to Rob all the way up to Port. The road's rocky in the National Park. There're potholes and loose dirt. But it's easy in Rob's four-wheel drive, except when we nearly hit a kangaroo. It just bounded across the track into the old ferns.

I like looking out of the car window at the huge ferns. There're crimson rosellas in the trees and pink-and-gray galahs. After everything happening with Mum, being here feels like pressure's slipping out of my head.

I spot some orangey banksia bushes. They make me think of dishes. "Hey, Rob, what's the same between the rainforest and you washing dishes?"

"Don't know, Jack."

"Both use bottle brushes."

"Ha-ha. I get it." Leo's laughing because he knows about Rob's nutty dishwashing too. Banksias look like a bottlebrush and Rob uses a bottle brush to get those dishes to shine.

There're squawky seagulls in the air as the road dips downward. Suddenly it appears like a movie. Blue waves with frothy white manes roll onto sandy beaches stretching out as far as we can see. Rob turns the four-wheel drive onto the sand and we coast along the beach with the salty smell of the ocean blowing through our open windows.

The campsite has a fire pit. We help Rob put up our tent. Leo and I collect wood, while Rob unpacks the car. When we come back, there're three folding chairs and a table around the fire pit. Rob brings out Mum's famous quiche and banana cake. Mum ... I get a lump in my throat. Then I see Rob's orange squisher and start to laugh. I explain it to Leo, who laughs too, as we squish and squeeze oranges. Rob can't go anywhere without his squisher.

"We'll catch flathead tomorrow."

I've got Grandad's fishing rod. I know I will.

Rob gives Leo a new fishing rod. "That's for you to keep, Leo."

"We might even catch blackfish. They're sweet if you cook them right."

The fire makes us warm. There are murmurs from another campsite and sounds from the bush. I like the *chit-chit* of the willie wagtail. The sun's setting across the beach and we eat, talk, tell jokes, and sleep really well in our tent.

Chapter 12

A Girl with a Bow in Her Hair

Mum loves the three blackfish we bring home. Samantha shows off that the girls' day out was fantastic. I'm glad they had a good time, but camping was the best.

Mum's still not doing jumping jacks and she starts treatment at the hospital soon.

When Christopher asks me to go over for dinner, I feel like I should stay home.

"Please go, Jack," Mum insists. "Say hello to them for me and tell them I'm doing well. I want you to have a good time. Rob and Nanna are home. Just go, please. Make me happy!"

I haven't had dinner there for ages. Christopher's

mother brings steamed bun dumplings stuffed with barbecued pork and vegetables. My favorite. There's noodle soup on the stove. I like that too.

"Enjoy." Christopher's mother smiles.

We talk about school, the bakery, my ponto, then Mum. "Mum's having radiation and she's doing OK."

"We are lucky to live in this country because there's treatment, doctors and hospitals. People can get better. Your mother'll get better." She pauses, looks at Christopher, then me. "There were women in my village who couldn't get treatment. There aren't many hospitals and medicines in Vietnam."

I find that unbelievable. After dinner Christopher and I look it up on the computer. *There are only two cancer centers; one in Hanoi in the north and one in Ho Chi Minh City in the south. This means only ten percent of the country's cancer needs are met. Breast cancer is one of the leading causes of cancer death in women in Vietnam. Yet with early diagnosis and appropriate treatment, breast cancer frequently has a good outcome.*

"Maybe we can do something, Christopher. Let's ask Mr. Angelou."

I can't sleep very well anymore. Samantha can't either. She asks if she can sleep in my room. I don't tell her that sharing makes me feel better too. I think everything is going to be all right. But I'm not sure. I'm glad Mum lives here where there're lots of hospitals. I'm going to ask Mr. Angelou about Vietnam. He'll have an idea.

School. In the break Mr. Angelou asks me how Mum is doing. He worries about Mum too. I wave to Christopher and Anna to come up and we explain about breast cancer and Vietnam. "Well, let's make it our charity this year. It'll be yellow daffodils for this school." As I look up at him, his bald head shines. He's the best teacher in the world, even when he's angry.

The Yellow Daffodil Cancer Cake Sale is a huge success. Anna organizes the other kids in our class to sell the cakes. Christopher's parents bake the cakes. Samantha and a few other kids make the posters:

Buy a Cake and
Save a Mum
from Breast Cancer
from Australia to Vietnam.

Yellow daffodils are on sale in the school administration and lots of kids are wearing them. The money from the daffodils goes to breast and other cancer research, and the cake-sale money goes to Médecins sans Frontières, which helps women in

Vietnam get cancer treatment. Mum is so proud of us.

Nanna's joined a new bridge club at the Senior Citizens' and is already a star. Everyone says she's a natural card player. I know that from playing UNO. They love her there. She's on the Senior Citizens' Organizing Committee within about five minutes. "Nanna may not be able to dance much anymore, but she's smart and wants to be useful. She's got to have a life that's not just only us," Mum says. The bus comes twice a week to pick up Nanna. She looks forward to it and Mum's happy.

Nanna loves the afternoon teas at bridge club. "The Senior Citizens' club has lovely scones with cream and jam or sometimes chocolate brownies." She always brings us home a scone or a brownie each.

Mum's into the third week of radiation. She's tired like Rob said. I help with the shopping and I even did the laundry yesterday. Mum works part time, has treatment, comes home. She needs to sleep in the afternoons. Today is Nanna's bridge day and it's a pupil-free day as well. That means no students at school and no Nanna at home. So Samantha and I are going with Mum to the radiation-oncology department.

We follow Mum inside the hospital. Mum knows exactly where to go, since she's been here nearly every day. She swings past the hospital administration, past pathology, waves at the radiation-oncology receptionist and goes into the waiting room. Everyone knows Mum and there are plenty of hellos. "These are my terrific children," Mum announces to the nurse. "Jack and Samantha." Wish Mum wouldn't do that. She fluffs her orange skirt and her hair out; she must be feeling better. The nurse smiles. "Heard all about you, Jack. How's the ponto growing?"

I hate Mum talking about me to everyone. "It's good," I grunt. Actually my ponto is nearly ready to eat. I've recorded and photographed every stage of its development. I've got three other pontos growing. I'm thinking of planting even more and setting up a ponto workbench in the workshop.

The nurse shows us a pile of books. "Help yourself, kids." Samantha finds a crossword book. She loves doing crosswords. I choose a book called *Cosmos* that looks "out of this world." Joke. Joke. There's a cart with apple juice, salad and cheese sandwiches cut into triangles, and coffee and tea. Mum pours juice for us. I take two sandwiches. Samantha does too. I drop into one of the comfortable couches while Samantha sprawls beside me. Mum gives her a pen for her crosswords.

I look around and feel relieved. It's pretty nice in here. There are quite a few people in the waiting room. Lots of different ages. A few are bald, even a lady. Mum is chatting to a grandma who's got purple dye on her knee. Mum knows her from other visits here. The waiting room has toys for kids. Samantha puts down her pen and sits on the floor next to a little girl who's playing with colored blocks. She needs help with the tower. As I check out what they're doing, the little girl looks up at me.

She's got large dark eyes like Anna's, but she hasn't got Anna's hair or much hair at all really. A satin pink ribbon is tied around her head with a bow at the side. There's purple dye on her head and I try doubly hard to make her laugh. We build a terrific castle with two towers when the little girl's mother approaches us. She smiles. "We have to go now." She takes the little girl's hand and they walk down the hallway to another room. The little girl waves goodbye.

We sit back on the couch with Mum. Samantha says, "That little girl is so cute. What's wrong with her?" I know what's wrong with her.

Mum looks down the hallway. "She has cancer and it's being treated, like mine is. Like the grandma I was speaking to."

"But she's lost her hair."

"That's the radiation on her head. Her hair will grow back." Samantha looks at Mum's blond fluff. "I won't lose my hair from this. If I have chemotherapy, then I could lose my hair for a while. Anyway I'm not having chemotherapy. I'm lucky."

Is Mum lucky? I stare at her and hope she's telling the truth this time.

"Will the little girl be all right?"

"She'll get better. I don't know for how long, but the treatment is helping her." Mum smiles. "I'm getting help too." Samantha hugs Mum. I really think Mum is getting better. That makes me feel better.

Mum looks at her watch. "Got to get ready. Have to change into my stunning white sack outfit. I'm going to look like a model again."

"You look good in anything, Mum."

"Flattery gets you everywhere, Jack."

Mum is in her white sack when she waves us over. "I've organized that you kids can have a quick look into the radiation treatment room." It is *super* quick, but it's interesting. Reminds me of a laboratory. There's a major X-ray machine like a big metal right angle, hanging over a metal bed. "OK, you've seen it now." Mum mouths *thank you* to the technician as she nudges us out. "I've got to go in now. So I'll see you both in around twenty minutes."

I have another apple juice. Samantha finishes another crossword and Mum's back in no time and she's laughing. All good. Now it's lunch and I'm ready for something real to eat. Afterward we're going to the movies. I love a day off school with Mum. We head for our regular hamburger cafe. "Order what you want," she announces. My hamburger has it all, with an egg, bacon, cheese, beets, salad, and ketchup and fries. Samantha just gets a plain hamburger with cheese, and fries of course. Mum's not very hungry, so she has a fruit salad and mineral water.

It's so good that Mum and Rob have finally set a new wedding date. It means Mum is going to be all right. The wedding will be after radiation therapy has finished in the school vacation. Invitations are being mailed soon. Some of the envelopes have little bits of leftover mouse poop on them. I secretly wipe the evidence away. People will just think it's a smudge from the post office.

The Napolis are designing a fruit platter display. "It'll be a work of art." Anna's so proud that I think she's going to pop like a balloon. Christopher's parents are baking the wedding cake with the wedding figures of Mum the hippie and Rob the surfer. I have to give some advice about the way they look. They were going to put white underpants on Rob — the nerdiest surfer in the world. Samantha gave them her boy surfer doll with cool board shorts. We saved the cake.

Nanna's bought a new dress. The rest of us have our wedding clothes ready, including Mum. Leo's coming down for a week and staying in my room. I don't care anymore that I'm going to look like a penguin. As long as Leo does too, it's fine. It'll be funny anyway. Everything is go, go, go. Rob's going to be my real stepdad. Samantha calls him Dad sometimes. Dad-Rob-Dad-Rob. Leo calls him Dad. Maybe. No, I'd better call him Rob.

Great news. No, great, great, *great* news. Mum's had her last radiation. Her breast is red and sore, but that'll disappear in a few weeks. My head doesn't hurt so much and I'm starting to sleep again. (Except I sometimes wake up with these dumb nightmares that Mum's gone.) Mum is nearly doing jumping jacks and she skips along the front path. We're having a party to celebrate.

Sunday party lunch. The Napolis arrive with a bowl that looks like vine leaves. It's filled with a huge serving of tomato-and-black-olive pasta. Anna's carrying a matching bowl, but it contains passion fruit and mangoes. It's sweet like … Oh no, my brain must be turning into mush. I was going to say "sweet like Anna." Luckily I didn't say it aloud.

Christopher throws his handball in the air, walking behind his parents. They baked a Vietnamese cake. "You'll enjoy this honeycomb cake. It's made with coconut milk." Nanna's very interested in the cake and chats to Christopher's mother about it.

Lunch is a feast. Mum made her famous egg-and-bacon quiche. Samantha and Anna made their famous banana cake with the mango yogurt — *Jack's* ingredient. Rob and I created our soon-to-be-famous salad. I included baby tomatoes, baby corn spears, baby asparagus and baby potatoes. Rob added baby spinach leaves. You guessed it. The famous secret is the "baby" ingredients. Nanna is the famous eater, except she complained that there were no chocolate chip cookies. Mum decorated the table with our famous sunflowers.

"Hey, Nanna, why did the cookie cry?"

Nanna tries to answer this as it's close to her heart and stomach. "Because there were no cookies at the party."

"Good try, Nanna, but that's wrong. Anyone else want to have a guess?"

There are a few crummy (Get it? Crummy?) replies. "Give up?" Everyone does. "The answer is … drumroll please," I tap the chair, "because its mother has been a wafer (Get it? Away for?) so long."

"That's a good one, Jack." Rob puts his hand on Mum's shoulder. "But Mum's back now."

"And she's back and well." Mr. Napoli lifts up his glass. "A toast." Everyone lifts their glass for Mum.

Mum stops Rob from doing the dishes. There are so many dishes as well. I'll be needed to help afterward. "Let's leave the dishes for later, Rob."

Then Mum whispers in his ear. Rob disappears into the backyard. Mum rounds up everyone in the family room. It's speech time. I'm sitting on the floor between Anna and Christopher when I notice Rob's head poking through the doorway. Mum waves her hands around and gets everyone's attention. "Thank you so much for your support. Now I know that I have the best friends in the world and the best family. It's been easier because of all of you." Mum's face lights up. "Rob and I have got something special for Samantha and Jack. It's a special thank you to our wonderful kids." Mum, please don't go on. Not in front of everyone. She looks at the door. Then she gives a nod to Rob who wanders in carrying a big brown box. "Samantha and Jack, please come up."

We're standing there like idiots when I notice something's moving in the big brown box. Samantha looks in. "Ooooohhh ... Oooohh ... Ooooohh ..."

I look in. "Oooooohhh ... Oooohh ... Ooooh ..."

He's white with brown patches and cute ears and a waggly tail.

We call him Ollie.

Chapter 13

Pooper-Scoopers

Samantha is throwing a ball to Ollie, except Samantha is catching the ball and Ollie's crazily licking her. Nanna's all smiles as she watches comfortably from a chair. Puss is watching from Nanna's window. Poor Puss. She's still trying to figure out what a puppy means and when it's safe to come out. Samantha's stopped drawing dog posters, but I have to take endless dog photos of Ollie. Luckily I like taking photos of Ollie because he's so funny.

Some hilarious moments: chasing his tail (he didn't catch it); wearing Nanna's yellow sun hat (he's part of the family now); chewing Mum's slipper (thought it was a rabbit, lucky it wasn't); asleep (with paws stuck in the air and totally stuffed). Floppy has a real live friend now. Ollie's barred from all rooms except the kitchen until he's house-trained. There have been some wet spots and a poop, but he's getting there. Can't wait to take him to the park this afternoon. He can join us for the hill slides. Anna and Christopher are coming, and of course, Samantha.

Christopher's early. I want to show him my ponto and the baby pontos. "It's scientifically recorded. Mr. Angelou said I should enter it in the Schools' Science Competition."

"You should, Jack."

With Mum being sick, I hadn't felt like doing that. But it's different now. "It's a monster," I tell Christopher. He inspects the ponto. I put the camera on a timer on my desk and race to stand beside Christopher. *Click* Photo taken.

Christopher's quieter than usual. He stands in front of Grandad's Vietnam War medals hanging in the cabinet.

"Are you all right?"

"I'm all right, but ..." He waits for a while. "Something has happened at home."

"Is everyone all right?"

"It's something good, but Mum and Dad don't want people to know yet. I asked if I could tell you." Since our Vietnam project and the Yellow Daffodil Cancer Cake Sale, we talk a lot more.

"What is it?"

"My parents got this letter from the Red Cross. They've been looking for so long." Christopher touches the glass display cabinet showing Grandad's medals. "My aunt. My mother's sister. The Red Cross has found her. She's alive, living in a village near Hanoi. My mother cried so much after the letter." He's breathless. "The stories of escaping on the fishing boat. Not knowing where her sister was. She's always felt very sad."

This is mind-blowing. Like Mum surviving cancer. "It's been so long since they escaped."

Christopher nods. "My mother never gave up. She's lit candles for her sister every Sunday."

"So what are you going to do?"

"Dad's going to work harder and keep the bakery open longer to get enough money for Mum to see her sister in Vietnam. He wants to save enough for all of us to go. And maybe one day she could come here."

"This is amazing."

Christopher smiles. "It is."

Samantha races into my room. "Anna's here." Mr. Napoli has dropped her off. "Come on, Jack. Ollie wants to go to the park."

We head for the kitchen and bump into Anna. "Hi, Christopher. Hi, Jack." She's standing next to four strong flat fruit boxes from Napolis' Super Delicioso Fruitologist Market. I reconstruct them back into boxes. Yes, they're looking good.

Christopher takes one box and I take another. "They're just right." He checks the box out.

Ollie will love the downhill box slides, but he doesn't love his leash. He keeps biting it until Samantha has to tap his nose. Ollie looks up with his doggy brown eyes at us, then charges ahead dragging Samantha behind him. Suddenly there's a stop-and-sniff spot. Oh no, poop on the neighbor's grass. That is a seriously bad thing about dogs. Anna's carrying a spade and bag. Scoop the poop. It's bagged and dumped in the nearest trash can. Lucky Anna's here. I don't want to be a pooper-scooper.

Ollie's on the move again, sniffing, running, dragging Samantha in the wrong direction. I carry Samantha's box. Finally we make it to the park and Ollie's let off his leash. He goes nuts running here and there and everywhere.

We all go to the top of the hill with our boxes. Ollie's barking after us. The grass is dry. Looks like a good run. I have a first try with everyone watching. My box is perched at the top. I give myself a send-off and *swoosh*, I'm belting down the hill with Ollie woofing behind me. I climb back up. "Come on. Your turn."

Samantha and Anna set up beside each other. I plonk Ollie into Samantha's arms. Christopher and I give each other the nod, then give a shove to the girls in their boxes. They're screaming. Ollie's ears are flapping. Oh no, Anna does an airborne hop over a clump of grass. She makes it. Samantha nearly crashes when Ollie wriggles out of her arms. And they're at the bottom. Christopher and I race down the hill to check that they're all right. They're laughing and Ollie is yapping. Yep, they're all right.

We slide down the hill heaps of times with Ollie barking, running, riding. I get some amazing shots of Samantha screaming, Christopher racing down the hill, Anna with her hair blowing in the wind. I repair Samantha's box twice and Anna's box once. Christopher writes his off when the bottom falls out on the last run. Boxes are getting wrecked and Samantha scrapes her knee. I look at my watch. We're ready to go.

I carry Ollie on the way home. He's puffed and stuffed. His tail is wagging in my ear. "Stop it, Ollie." Suddenly there's a huge slurp.

Christopher's laughing. "You don't need a shower tonight." Samantha pats him and Anna takes Ollie for a long hug. He is one spoiled puppy.

Mum's waiting for us with water and food for Ollie and water and food for us. She takes me aside.

"Christopher's mother called me. It's such good news, isn't it?"

Everything's looking good.

Mum's last checkup. The doctor says the tumor is gone and she's healing. She has to go back in three months' time for a checkup and later a mammogram. There are pills to take every day for five years to help prevent it coming back. I just know that Mum's going to be all right. It's the best day of my life.

Mum's back at full-time work. She postpones her library degree until next year, but she's determined to finish it. I enter my ponto in the Science Competition. Mr. Angelou is happy about that. Everyone is happy about that, except it makes me nervous. What if no one thinks it's good enough? What if no one cares about my ponto?

Anna whispers to me when I hand it to Mr. Angelou, "Your ponto will win, Jack. It's incredible. I'm so proud of you."

I wish Anna hadn't said that to me. I pretend it doesn't matter, but I've worked so hard on it. I'll probably lose. "It's nothing, Anna. I'm just entering it for Mr. Angelou. That's all." Please, please let me get a prize.

Nanna wins the "Most Improved Bridge Player" at the Seniors' and gets an award. It's a gold column with a shield at the top with Nanna's name on it. Mum puts it on the mantelpiece.

Ollie stops pooping and peeing in the kitchen. So now he's allowed in the rest of the house. Frank and Spot freak out. I can't move the mouse-house into Nanna's room because Puss lives in there. Mum won't allow them in Rob and her bedroom because she still doesn't like mice. Samantha has Ollie in her room all the time. My rat, Hector, is going to have to get used to Frank and Spot.

The wedding. It's the main topic of conversation. We're having a family meeting tonight to discuss the wedding *again*. The invitations haven't even been mailed. No one's going to be here if they don't get invitations.

Ollie is chewing his soft, furry, black-and-white bone. He took a bite out of Floppy's ear, and got into huge trouble. Floppy's on Samantha's shelf now with a bandage on his head. Puss is safe in Nanna's lap. Rob strips off his yellow rubber gloves. He's finished the dishes. Hurry up. Hurry up.

Mum starts at last. "Christopher's parents have had wonderful news." We all know now. Let's get on to the wedding. I'm still setting up my baby ponto plantation and want to get to the workshop. "Christopher is one of your best friends, Jack."

Where is this going? "As a family I'd like to ask you if we can make the wedding extra special."

Mum gives Rob a look. He takes over. "You might be wondering why the invitations haven't been sent out yet." I nod. "The invitations are from all of us and the wedding is going to be a great party. But we want it to be more than that. People are going to bring presents. Mum and I have thought about this seriously. We'd like to ask them *not* to bring a gift, but to donate money for three tickets to Vietnam. For Christopher and his parents."

It takes a while to think about what Rob's said. It's such a great idea.

Nanna takes out her handkerchief to wipe her eyes. "Grandad's here," she mumbles. Grandad would like this.

Samantha nods so hard that Ollie starts yapping again.

This feels so right. "It's going to be the best wedding ever, Mum."

"I think it will be, Jack."

Leo arrives. He's impressed with my pontos. We go to the beach most days. Anna comes sometimes, but it's different from when it's just Anna and me. Christopher meets us when he's not helping in the bakery. Paul and my other friends bring their boards.

Rob's driving us to the beach today because Nanna's coming, as well as Ollie. There's a leash-free play area and special pooper-scooper trash cans.

"Come on, kids," Mum calls out. Rob gets a great parking spot, but we're never getting into the water. It's Nanna. She's stuck in the back seat and can hardly get out. I can't find my camera until I look at Nanna. It's under her. "I wondered why the seat was so lumpy." She rubs her bottom and there's a flash of purple.

"Aren't those underpants too hot?"

"They're just perfect and the right price."

Quickly I set up the sun umbrella and a folding chair for Nanna. She's watching my camera. "And *please* don't sit on it, Nanna."

Ollie's already in the dog play area with Samantha and Mum. The waves are gently curling. Leo and I race into the surf. The first shock of the water is cold, but then it's perfect. Leo catches a wave that goes right onto the beach. "You're good, Leo." He half-kneels and shows us a few tricks before paddling toward a new set of waves. "Glad about your mum." He paddles beside me to say this. Then he turns, paddling into the wave. Leo is all right.

Chapter 14

The Wedding

Day before the wedding. It's a military operation. Rob is the general. I'm the lieutenant. Leo and Samantha are aides. Anna's coming to organize the flowers. Mum's finalizing the wedding celebrant, the order of events, guest list, food. Nanna's helping Mum. She's taste-testing the sweet treats. Ha-ha.

The tent arrives and Rob sets up its location. Samantha and I lay out the chairs and drag in the podium. Rob and I roll the red carpet down the middle of the chairs to make an aisle. Anna arrives. The Napolis have sent bucket-loads of cut flowers. The sunflowers in the garden splash yellow at the side of the podium.

Wedding morning. Wedding cake arrives from Christopher's bakery. Fruit platters arrive from the

Napolis. Mum's friend who's a hairdresser has been doing hair and makeup since seven this morning. Rob and I are lucky. Our prickle heads are just right. Wedding clothes are laid out in everyone's room.

One o'clock. Nearly there. Mum's in her bedroom with Samantha doing the final touches. Nanna's having a quick nap before the ceremony. Rob's in a large penguin suit with a sunflower-yellow shirt and multicolored bow tie. Leo's in a small penguin suit with a matching sunflower-yellow shirt and bow tie. I am too. Rob and Leo go to the front porch to talk. The wedding starts at three o'clock.

Anna floats into the family room in her bridesmaid dress. She's so beautiful that I can hardly breathe. "Let's go into the garden," her musical voice sings. "You look handsome, Jack." I feel my face go hot. The garden is quiet now. It feels odd after all the noise and setting up. Anna shows me her flower arrangements. When she bends to smell the white jasmine, her black ringlets fall between the flowers. We talk for ages. I take her hand. My heart's throbbing and then she kisses me on the cheek.

Guests are arriving. Oh, there's Mr. Angelou wearing a blue suit. Makes him look bigger, especially with his bald head. He calls me over and says quietly in my ear, "It's not announced, but there's good news about your ponto. It's shortlisted. We'll talk more later." Anna, the ponto, Mum and Rob splash into my mind. This is such a great day.

There are lots of envelopes dropped in the gift collection box for Christopher's family. Ollie's got a bow tie around his neck that matches mine. He's being hopeless, chewing the chair covers. Rob's tied him up with a long rope to a pole in the garden. Puss is watching from Nanna's window.

Oh, Nanna. Here she comes. I can't believe it. She's wearing a flouncy purple skirt. I run up to her and kiss her. "You look beautiful, Nanna." I just know she's wearing her purple underpants. She shows me her locket pinned to her blouse. I open it. There's Grandad. It feels as though he's here.

Everyone is seated. Christopher's mother is wearing a flowing emerald áo-dài. The celebrant, who's a lady dressed in silvery-gray, is facing the guests at the podium. Rob and Leo are standing at the front. The music starts. Anna and Samantha are holding posies of yellow roses and slowly walking down the red carpet. Mum's waiting in the house. Her hair falls in soft curls around a daisy chain. Her dress is like summer, covered with sunflowers and sparkles. She *is* summer and I know she's going to be my mum for a long time.

"Jack, are you ready to give me away?"

I nod, and take Mum's arm, and walk her down the aisle.

Famous Banana Cake	Jack's Notes
½ cup soft butter	Don't melt it
½ cup castor sugar	Castor means super-fine sugar
2 large eggs, beaten	Try eggs from a farm — free range
2 large, ripe bananas, mashed or 3 small ones	Napolis' squishy bananas
1½ cups self-rising flour	Tall flour (Jack joke)
½ teaspoon baking soda	Have a burp here (Great Jack joke)
pinch salt	Don't pinch too hard (Another great Jack joke)
¼ cup milk	Mum likes low-fat milk
2 tablespoons mango yogurt	Your favorite yogurt is good if you don't like mango

How to Make the Cake

Cream butter and sugar until light and fluffy.

Beat in eggs a bit at a time into the sugary, creamy butter.

Stir in half the flour, baking soda and all the mashed bananas.

Fold in the rest of the flour, baking soda and milk, making it smooth. Then stir in the yogurt.

Spoon mixture into a greased 8" x 4" loaf pan or 8" round cake pan.

Cook Banana Cake

Bake at 350°F for about 40 minutes, or until cooked.

Cool cake for 5 minutes in pan before turning out.

Jack's Job: Eat Banana Cake

Have a slice, and then another slice and share around. Yum.

Acknowledgments

Cancer Council NSW, Australia, is a special organization dedicated to defeating cancer. As well as funding more cancer research than any other charity in the state, it advocates for the highest quality of care for cancer patients and their families, and empowers people with knowledge about cancer, its prevention and early detection. I would especially like to thank Julie Callaghan and Kendra Sundquist from Cancer Council for their great support.

I would also like to acknowledge the generous contribution of the National Breast and Ovarian Cancer Center (www.nbocc.org.au) for providing expert advice in the development of *Always Jack*.

There's a special embrace to my friends who have been through the journey. Some are survivors — Inga Gray, Sharon Rundle and Lynne Celler — while others have passed on to another life — Sandy Campbell, Eileen Collins and my beloved father, Zoltan Gervay.

Another thank you goes to my beautiful family and friends for their love and support during difficult times, as I am a multiple cancer survivor.

I would also like to thank my Australian publisher, Lisa Berryman, for her support.

I wrote *Always Jack* for the children, so they know that they are loved and that their community cares for them.

"Susanne Gervay's *Always Jack* makes it safe for children, parents and the wider community to talk about cancer."
— Cancer Council NSW

www.cancercouncil.com.au

I live near the beach and I love my kids. You'll meet them in my Jack books. You'll also meet their Nanna who wobbles, and when she coughs her teeth fall out. I invite everyone into my family and community. Jack, inspired by my son, is warm, funny, quirky and real. You'll know Jack. He's your neighbor, friend, brother or you. He tells great jokes. Well, he thinks he does.

I wrote *I Am Jack* after my son won the battle against school bullying. It's been adapted into an acclaimed play by Monkey Baa Theatre and has become an important no-to-bullying book. How special is that? I wrote *SuperJack* when our family blended, to make it OK for kids to talk about new parents and siblings. I feel that's special too.

Now I've written *Always Jack*. *Jack* makes you laugh, love and play, but also reaches into big issues such as cancer, divorce, grandparents, sibling rivalry, friendships, refugees and the Vietnam War.

At its heart, I wrote *Always Jack* so that kids and families can really talk. As a multiple breast cancer survivor myself, *Always Jack* makes kids safer.

Part survival manual, part therapy, part autobiography, part fiction, *Always Jack* carries the Australian Cancer Council's endorsement and my love.

Suzanne Gervay
www.sgervay.com
www.sgervay.com/blog